IN THE LAND OF THE
LAWN WEENIES

AND OTHER WARPED AND
CREEPY TALES

Don't get left behind!

STARSCAPE

Let the journey begin . . .

IN THE LAND OF THE LAWN WEENIES

AND OTHER WARPED AND CREEPY TALES

DAVID LUBAR

STARSCAPE

A TOM DOHERTY ASSOCIATES BOOK
NEW YORK

This is a work of fiction. All the characters and events portrayed in this book are either products of the author's imagination or are used fictitiously.

IN THE LAND OF THE LAWN WEENIES AND OTHER WARPED AND CREEPY TALES

Copyright © 2003 by David Lubar

The Psychozone: Kidzilla & Other Tales © 1996 by David Lubar
The Psychozone: The Witch's Monkey & Other Tales © 1997 by David Lubar

A Starscape Book
Published by Tom Doherty Associates, LLC
175 Fifth Avenue
New York, NY 10010

www.starscapebooks.com

ISBN: 0-765-34570-6

First Starscape edition: June 2003

Printed in the United States of America

0 9 8 7 6 5 4 3 2 1

For Mom,
who always had the time for a trip to the library
and
for Alison,
who had to read these stories because I'm her
Dad and I said so.

CONTENTS

CONTENTS

IN THE LAND OF THE
LAWN WEENIES

AND OTHER WARPED AND
CREEPY TALES

FAIRY IN A JAR

▼

You probably think of fairies, if you think of them at all, as wonderful little creatures flying happily through the forest, dancing and singing and making merry. Let me tell you something: Fairies might look lovely on the outside, but inside they are ugly, real ugly. Fairies are mean and vicious. They've got teeth like tiny needles. One bite wouldn't hurt much. But I'm pretty sure they wouldn't stop at one; they'd keep biting and chewing until they hit something vital. Fairies aren't good news. I know. Let me tell you about my fairy in a jar.

I'd been running around the backyard trying to catch fireflies with the net from this bug kit I'd gotten years ago. The kit was a birthday present from an aunt who had no idea what I liked. I might have used it once or twice, but mostly it just sat at the back of my closet under a pile of other junk. I'd lost the collecting bottle that came with it, but I found an old jar and punched a couple of holes in the lid. Bugs probably didn't need much air, but it was fun banging away with a hammer and nail. Anyhow, I was swiping the net at some bugs because there was nothing on TV except reruns and all my friends were busy and I couldn't find anything else to do.

I'd caught a couple fireflies and put them in the jar. The whole adventure was getting boring pretty fast. I was just about to quit when I saw a flash under the birch tree at the back of the yard near the woods. Thinking about it later, I sort of remember that the flash was different. It was more glittery, almost a sparkle.

I crept over and swung the net.

Thunk! Something heavy hit the bottom. I jumped. I thought I'd caught a bat. My skin crawled at that idea. I fumbled the jar lid open and slammed the net down. I felt a solid plunk against the glass. *Got it,* I thought. I needed two tries to get the lid on right. The jar kept shaking in my hand. So did the lid.

A bat. My very own bat. The guys would go wild when I showed it to them.

I held the jar up to see my catch. Three fireflies were crawling around the sides. But that wasn't what grabbed my attention. There was something else crumpled on the bottom. It wasn't a bat—not even close. It wasn't an *it,* either. It was a she.

She unfolded herself and rose slowly to her feet, shimmering in the light of the quarter moon. She was no more than five inches tall. Skinny. Long dark hair. Green dress. Wings. She looked down at her body, as if checking for injuries. The jar was still shaking in short jerks that made her stagger and fight for balance. She pressed her hands against the glass and stared straight at me. For an instant, so quick I thought at first it was my imagination, there was nothing in her gaze but pure hatred.

Then she smiled.

Maybe I should have smashed the jar against the tree. Maybe I should have smashed it and run—just run and run forever. "Maybe" isn't worth much—it's only a word. In a way, I understood how that kid at the playground must have felt last week when I punched him in the gut. Everything inside of me was stunned. I felt that my body had been filled with glue. I held the jar and stared at her.

"*Let me go, kind sir.*" Her voice was like bells and dreams and whispers in my mind.

I grabbed the lid. I started to twist it loose, but that look of hate flashed across her face again. I knew. In that thousandth of a second, I knew I could never set her free. By then, I also knew I didn't want to set her free. She was mine. I had captured a prize no one else could even imagine.

"*Wishes,*" she said. "*I can grant wishes.*"

That got my interest. I took my hand off the lid and held it out, palm up. "Show me. A thousand dollars. Right here." I wiggled my fingers.

"*You have to free me first.*"

"I don't think so." I wasn't stupid. I wasn't going to fall for some sort of trick.

"That is the rule." Her voice grew colder.

"I make the rules now." It felt good to say that.

"Please."

"No."

Still staring at me, she flicked her hand out and grabbed one of the fireflies from the side of the jar.

Still staring at me, she raised the struggling insect to her mouth.

Still staring, she bit off the head of the firefly.

I don't know if she kept staring after that. I looked away. But I squeezed the jar, as if to make sure the glass was strong enough to keep her trapped. It was one of those jars people put home-made stuff in. The lady next door had this wormy old apple tree. Each year she made applesauce for the whole neighborhood. Every house got a jar, tied with a red ribbon. No one ever eats it. We just toss out the whole thing, or dump the sauce and keep the jar. The glass felt solid. It would hold her.

I took the jar up to my room, being careful that nobody saw it. I put it on the top shelf in my closet.

The next morning, I almost convinced myself none of it had happened. Almost. But the jar was there. And she was there. At first I thought she was dead. She was crumpled on the bottom again. Then, as I saw her let out a shallow breath, I realized she was sleeping—sleeping or in some sort of suspended state. *Creature of the night.* I don't know where that phrase came from, but it ran through my head. I noticed something else. The bugs were gone—all three of them. *Bon appetit.*

I shook the jar a bit, but she just slid around without waking. I could wait. She'd be up after dark. I was pretty sure of that. Somehow, some way, I was going to get a payoff from her.

Sure enough, when I checked that night, she was awake, sitting on the bottom of the jar. "Good evening," I said, speaking quietly so nobody would hear me talking in my room.

"Set me free. I shall reward you with wonders beyond your imagining." She looked up at me and smiled. A chill ran down my spine.

"Cut the babble and give me some details. What can you do?" I picked up the jar, holding the sides of the lid. Even protected by the glass, I didn't want to put my fingers too close to her.

"Whatever you wish."

I didn't believe her. Promises were easy to make. "Show me."

"Free me first."

I shook my head. It was a standoff, but I was the one with the power. She was mine. She would give me something valuable. She had no choice. I owned her now. "Think about it," I said, putting the jar back on the shelf. "Think of some way to buy your freedom. I'm sure you'll come up with an idea."

She gave me that look again, and a flash of those teeth. I closed the closet door and left the room. The next day, we had the same conversation, and the same again on the day after. I wanted proof. She wanted freedom. But she was weakening. I could see that. I knew she had to give me a reward sooner or later. I could wait. I was in charge.

On the fifth day, she agreed to my request. *"I will transmute an object for you,"* she said. Her voice was thinner, barely louder than a thought.

"Transmute?"

"I will change its form. Give me carbon. I will make a diamond."

"A diamond? That's more like it." I wondered for a moment how I was going to sell a diamond. But that problem could wait. Right now, I needed some carbon. That was easy enough. Charcoal for the grill, that was carbon. So was the graphite in pencils. So were diamonds. They were all just different forms of carbon. I couldn't believe that something I learned in Mr. Chublie's stupid science class was actually worth knowing. Live and learn. But I wasn't about to try to stick a big hunk of charcoal in the jar. There was no way I was opening that lid, not even for a second. I wasn't falling for any of her tricks. As I looked around the room, I saw the answer right next to me.

I yanked out my desk drawer and hunted around the sides and corners. "Got it." Perfect. I knew I had it in there—a whole pack of refills for my mechanical pencil. The best part was that they were thin enough to slip through the air-holes in the lid of the jar. I was planning to keep a nice, solid barrier between me and those teeth, thank you.

She gathered the pieces of lead. *"This will take some time."*

"I can wait."

She sat staring at the slivers of carbon. I put the jar away for the night. In the morning, I rushed to the closet to see my first diamond. In my head, I'd already spent the money—a new bike, new sneakers, all the new video games. The guys were definitely going to envy me.

But she wasn't finished. The pieces of lead were still there, though they looked smaller and shinier than before. *"It takes time,"* she said.

I would have to be patient.

"It takes time," she warned again that evening.

I waited. On the fourth night, she was done. *"Here."* She held up her hand. *"Take this and set me free."*

"What are you trying to pull?" I almost smashed the jar. There was nothing more than the tiniest sparkle in her tiny hand. She had made a miniature diamond chip. It was worthless. My dreams of wealth turned pale and vanished.

"This is all I can give you. Take it and set me free. You made a bargain."

I was so disgusted, I just put the jar back in the closet and went to bed. Maybe I heard something that night. I can't remember. I'm too scared to really remember. But I remember the morning. Every second is burned into my brain.

I got up. I walked to the closet. The door was open about an inch. I'd thought I'd closed it. I opened it all the way and reached for the jar. My hand stopped. My breath stopped. My heart almost stopped. There was a hole in the side of the jar. There was a round piece of glass on the shelf next to the jar. She was gone.

How? Then I knew. The diamond. She'd tricked me. She knew I wouldn't take that tiny diamond. She also knew it could cut through the glass.

She was free. Somewhere, she was sleeping. But night was coming. And she would wake. And she would come for me.

I'm afraid to go to sleep tonight. I don't think I will ever sleep again.

THE TOUCH

▼

Laura thought a flea market would be fun. It sounded wonderful. "There'll be all kinds of things to see," her mom had said. "You'll love it."

But it was just a bunch of junk—nothing but a lot of people sitting around in the hot sun trying to sell things that nobody wanted. It was boring. The buyers looked bored. The sellers looked bored. Even the stuff being sold looked bored. And every five seconds her mom would warn her "Don't touch" or "Look with your eyes, not your hands, Laura."

Right. Like she really wanted to touch any of that junk. She'd have to wash her hands for a week to get them clean after putting her fingers on any of this stuff. Laura looked at the table in front of her. There was a box of moldy books—

the same books everyone else was selling. There was another box with record albums. *Records,* Laura thought. *Who in the world would want those ancient things?* There was a ratty old doll with a stained dress and a chip missing from her cheek. Her hair was tangled and stiff. *Yuk,* Laura thought.

"Mom, can we go now? Pleeeeeaaase."

"In a minute," her mom muttered. She was studying an old butter dish like it was the lost treasure of ancient Egypt.

Sure. Laura knew what "in a minute" meant. She was doomed. She searched the table again, desperately hoping to see something that would hold her interest for a moment or two. She glanced at the woman in the folding chair behind the table. She must have been ninety years old. She was sitting there, staring off to one side, paying no attention to the items she'd set out for sale.

Laura shivered and looked back at the table. Dancing light sparkled in the sun as Laura moved her head. Her eyes were treated to a flash of red, followed by rainbow bursts. Laura gasped. Right in front of her, nearly lost among the rusty tools and cracked dishes and rotted magazines, was the most beautiful, unexpected treasure.

Could it be? Laura stepped closer, pressing against the edge of the table. Her hand darted out, then stopped halfway. She glanced to the left. Her mom had put down the butter dish and was examining a tarnished fork. Laura gazed back toward the crystal horse. It was the most lovely thing she had ever seen. The sight brought back memories of a merry-go-round she had ridden long ago. Every detail was carved in this ornament—the flying mane, the ribbon-covered pole, the fancy saddle. Laura could almost hear the music and feel the rise and fall of the horse as they rode in circles on a summer day.

She glanced around again. Her mom wasn't looking. The old lady wasn't looking. Laura had to touch that sparkling crystal treasure. It was calling her. She reached out to pick it up. She lifted it.

She felt a snap.

A leg broke. It fell with a small tinkle to the table. Laura froze. She waited for the shouting. There was nothing. The flea market buzzed on around her as if she hadn't just destroyed the most beautiful jewel in the world. Trying not to attract attention, Laura lowered the crystal horse to the table. It started to fall as she put it down, tilting toward where the leg had been. She leaned it against the side of the doll with the chipped cheek.

"Mom, can we go?"

Her mother sighed. "All right, but don't ask me to bring you here again."

No problem, Laura thought as she moved from the table. She hurried away, but a burning feeling in the back of her neck made her spin around. Behind her, the woman slowly turned her head toward Laura. She looked right at her. She looked right *through* her. The woman raised her left hand. She touched her left palm with her right forefinger.

Laura watched, not understanding, wanting to explain that it wasn't her fault.

The woman flung her arms apart. Laura jumped. The woman laughed, then whispered several words.

Laura's fingers tingled. She glanced toward the horse. It wasn't there. The woman's laugh echoed in her head. Laura fled to her mom.

That night, when she went to bed, Laura was sure she was going to have nightmares about the flea market. "Sweet dreams," her mom said as she turned out the light. Laura waited until her mom left the room. Then, feeling just a bit childish, she rushed to her closet and hunted for Mister Hoppy. In the dim glow of the light from the hallway, she searched for the stuffed animal that she had slept with when she was little. It was silly, but she knew she needed Mister Hoppy tonight.

"There you are," she said when she spotted the stuffed rabbit with the bright blue eyes and floppy ears. As she picked it up, her hand tingled for a second.

She had no dreams that night.

When she woke the next morning, the flea market itself seemed almost a dream. Feeling foolish about her fears, Laura reached to put Mister Hoppy back in the closet.

"What the . . . ?" She couldn't find the bunny. It must have fallen to the floor. She looked. It wasn't on the floor. It wasn't under the bed or tangled in the sheets. It was just gone.

It has to be here somewhere, Laura thought. She knew she'd find it later.

Laura went down the stairs and into the

kitchen. A wonderful smell greeted her. "Waffles," she said when she saw what her mom was making. "My favorite."

"Just in time for breakfast, sleepyhead," her mom said. "I was getting ready to wake you."

Laura grabbed a plate from the cabinet and went over to the counter. "There you go," her mom said, lifting the hot, crispy treat out of the waffle iron. "By the way, I'm expecting an important call this morning, so don't tie up the phone."

"Yes, Mom." Laura carried her breakfast to the table. The waffle looked perfect. She could already imagine how fabulous it would taste. As she set the plate down, the waffle started to slide off. She stopped it with her free hand. There was a small tingle in her fingers. Laura let go of the plate and went to get the syrup.

"My word," her mom said. "You really wolfed that one down. You must have been starving. Would you like another?"

"What?" Laura was puzzled by the question. She walked back across the room and looked down at her plate. It was empty.

"Would you like another waffle?" her mom asked again.

Laura nodded. *This can't be happening,* she thought. She touched the plate and waited for the tingle. Nothing. She touched the table. Nothing. She thought about Mister Hoppy. Had he vanished like the waffle? *Did it only happen to important things?* Laura had to find out. She needed to touch something she cared about. She jumped from her seat. The chair crashed over as she ran to the living room.

"Laura!" her mom called after her.

What can I try? Laura wondered. There, on the table—the book she was reading. It was her favorite series. She touched it. Nothing—no tingle. She ran to the playroom. She started grabbing, touching, feeling—new toys, old toys. Nothing.

"Laura!" Her mom gripped her shoulder and spun her around. "What is it? What's wrong?"

Laura clutched her mother's hand, wondering how she could possibly explain. "Mom—" She stopped. There was a tingle.

"What is it?"

Laura was afraid to look away. She knew what would happen the second she took her eyes off her mother.

The phone rang.

"Stay there. I'll be right back." Her mother pulled free of Laura's grip and dashed from the room.

"Wait!" Laura shouted as she rushed after her. She stumbled over one of the toys she'd dropped. She caught her balance and raced toward the doorway.

"Mom!" Laura called.

The phone kept ringing in the kitchen. It rang and rang, unanswered. The ringing filled the room ahead of her.

Laura burst into the kitchen. There was no one there. She was alone.

Laura curled into a ball and grabbed her head in both hands and screamed. And through her screams, through the pounding fear that seized her mind and the shaking tremors that tore through every muscle of her body, she felt a tingle in her fingers where they touched her face.

The ringing stopped.

AT THE WRIST

▼

It wasn't my fault that Dad cut his hand off. I can't take any of the blame for that. Okay, I was in the room at the time, but I didn't do anything to startle him. He cut his hand off all by himself. As he would have said if I had done it, that was one bonehead move, one really stupid stunt.

He sort of messed up the workshop, too. But Dad probably won't be doing much woodworking in the future, and I certainly don't have any urge to tangle with power tools. I think some of them try to get you.

Okay, I guess I've made the point that none of it was my fault. At least, not Dad's accident. But then I had an accident of my own. When the guys from the ambulance came, they rushed away with Dad as fast as they could. Right after they left, I noticed that they'd forgotten to take his hand. I knew that the doctors could put it back on. Doctors do that kind of stuff on television all the time. It's called microsurgery. It's no big deal.

So I got some ice from the freezer and put it in the little cooler—the one Dad fills with soda when he's going out to a ball game. I got a bag from the drawer and grabbed the hand through the plastic. It felt kind of weird, like taking a steak out of the refrigerator, except it wasn't cold. Trying not to think about what I was doing, I picked up the hand and put it in the cooler. Then I put in more ice. As I was shutting the lid, the phone rang. I ran to the living room and answered the call. It was my friend Carl. I told him I didn't have time to talk. I hung up the phone and went back to the kitchen. The cooler had popped open, so I shut the lid again. Then I jumped on my bike and pedaled to the hospital.

But somewhere along the way, between the time I picked up the hand and the time I got to the hospital, I must have messed up. When the nurse opened the cooler, there was nothing in it except for the ice.

I'd lost Dad's hand.

This was not good. I went back to the house. On the way, I looked over the whole route I'd taken, hoping to spot the hand. No sign of it. I searched the house. Not a trace. Mom came back from the hospital and started looking. Even the cat sort of helped to look. At least, he sniffed around a lot. None of it did any good. We all came up empty handed.

"Well, where did you have it last?" Mom asked.

If I knew that, it wouldn't be lost, I thought, but I didn't say anything. I figured I was in enough trouble already. That wasn't really fair since I'd been trying to do a good deed.

As hard as we looked, we couldn't find the hand. After a few hours, it became a dead issue, to use a rather sick phrase. They can only sew stuff back if it's still in good condition. A hand doesn't keep very well if it isn't cold.

Dad came home two days later, but he didn't speak to me very much. I guess he was angry about his hand getting lost, but I don't see how it could have been my fault.

Another week passed. That's when it started. I was falling asleep, just drifting, not really asleep yet but definitely close. All of a sudden, out of nowhere, WHACK! Something smacked me on the butt so hard I thought my head would pop off.

I sat up fast, one hand reaching down to rub my stinging flesh. There was nobody in the room.

I thought I heard a faint scurrying, like someone scratching at a rug. But I wasn't listening very carefully. I was too busy trying to ignore the pain in my rear. It felt like I'd been hit by the world's champion of butt-smacking.

I looked around the table at breakfast the next morning, suspecting everyone but knowing that nobody there could have done it. Dad was still pretty weak. Mom was no powerhouse. My brother Ed was a runt, and my sister Darlene was only three. She could have hit me with all her strength and I might not have noticed.

"Something wrong?" Mom asked when she caught me staring.

"Nope," I lied. "Everything is fine."

"Fine for you," Dad muttered as he tried to butter a piece of toast. He'd been making a lot of comments like that the last few days. I half expected him to take me to the woods any time now and leave me stranded, or drown me in a sack in the lake like an unwanted kitten.

Nope, I decided it wasn't any of them. I was beginning to think that I'd imagined the whole thing. I'd been almost asleep. And there was no bruise or anything. I hadn't checked until morning, and it's not all that easy looking at your own butt in a mirror, but there certainly was no sign that anything had actually smacked me.

Real or not, it happened again the next night. This time, I was asleep. At least, I was asleep until I felt the smack. It was quickly followed by a second whack. I rolled over and sat up fast.

There was no one in the room.

I held my breath and listened for the scurrying sound. There was definitely something crawling across the room and scrabbling out the door. It was fast. In a moment, it had reached the hallway. Then the sound changed as the thing moved over the wooden floorboards.

I think, when I heard the sound of fingernails on wood, I began to suspect what I was dealing with. But I didn't want to face that possibility. I just didn't want to believe that Dad's hand had come back to punish me.

Nothing happened that night. But, two days

later, after taking a couple of hard swipes on the rump, I almost managed to catch hold of it. For an instant, our fingers met. There was no doubt. It was a hand. I couldn't identify it for sure as Dad's hand, though it was definitely big and kind of hairy. I doubted there were other hands out there itching with an urge to smack me.

Two thoughts crossed my mind. First, I had to do something to stop this or I'd end up spending the rest of my life avoiding hard chairs. But second, I wondered if the hand could still be re-attached. If it could move and spank and every-thing, maybe it could work normally if it was sewn back on Dad's wrist. I didn't know for sure. Hey, I'm not a doctor. But it certainly seemed worth a try.

So I started waiting for the hand at night. I'd lie there, pretending to sleep, making my breathing do that slow pattern that sounds like someone off in slumberland. It took a week, but finally, as I waited, I heard the click of nails on the wood in the hall followed by a creak as my door swung open. The scratching sound on the rug moved closer and closer to my bed.

I dove to the floor and made a grab, but the hand just managed to dodge from my clutches. I saw it dash through the doorway. I followed, run-ning down the hall.

"What's all the noise about?" Dad asked, looking out from his bedroom.

"Your hand!" I shouted, pointing toward the steps.

Dad must have caught sight of it, because he

joined in the chase. We ran down the steps. I nearly fell, but I managed to stay on my feet. The hand was just ahead of us. It went straight for the front hall. We had this cat door at the bottom of the regular door. The hand went right through it.

Dad and I followed the hand out to the yard.

"Got to catch it," I said.

"Yeah," Dad said.

The hand went around the side of the house and headed for the dock. We lived right next to a lake. We'd moved there because Dad liked to fish. He hadn't fished much in the last few weeks. We nearly caught up with the hand as it scampered toward the end of the dock.

"Stop," I shouted.

For an instant, the hand paused, as if listening to me. Then it dove into the water. Dad and I ran to the edge of the dock. We could see the hand swimming away.

"Come on," Dad said. He jumped into our little boat. I joined him. The motor had a pull cord. I guess Dad couldn't handle it too well. He just pointed at it. I stepped past him and yanked the cord. The engine roared to life. I cranked it up to full speed and raced after the hand.

I guess it would have been better if I had waited for Dad to sit down. As I gunned the engine and turned the boat, Dad fell into the water. Then, when I tried to go back to help, the boat sort of went over him.

It's a good thing I'd taken that lifesaving course last year. By the time I got Dad onto the dock, Mom had called an ambulance. It could have been worse. He didn't get hit on the head or anything. But the blade from the propeller had cut him pretty badly. Actually, it had cut his foot right off. There was no chance of finding the foot in the water. But I had a pretty strong suspicion I'd be seeing it again. And feeling it.

CRIZZLES

▼

"**N**ever let yourself get caught alone with a crizzle," Danny's grandpa told us that evening. It was the first thing he'd said to me since I'd arrived at Danny's place two hours earlier. Up until then, he'd just sat in his chair and stared out the window.

I looked at Danny, puzzled. He looked back at me and shrugged, then asked his grandpa, "What's a crizzle?"

"It's an awful thing," his grandpa said. "Looks just like a person. On the *outside*, that is. Looks just like you or me." He pointed at Danny, then at himself. "But inside, it's all dark and hungry. A crizzle lives for just one thing. A crizzle lives to get you alone and chomp your bones."

"How interesting," I said. "But we're a little old for fairy stories." I was hoping that he'd go back to ignoring us. I was in no mood to listen to him or any other adult. It was bad enough that I'd gotten into a fight with my folks. They're always bossing me around, and they're always trying to make me eat things I don't like. I can't believe the disgusting foods adults gobble up.

Well, I was sick of it, and I told them how I felt. Then Mom said if I didn't like it, I could find someone else to feed me. I was so angry I walked right out of the house with no idea where I was going. I'm not stupid, though—I grabbed a bag of cookies on the way through the kitchen. No way I was planning to go hungry.

I'd kept walking for a long time—long enough to eat all the cookies. I was almost at the edge of town when I realized how tired I was. But there was Danny's house, sitting at the end of the last side street before the woods. I barely knew him well enough to stop by, but he seemed happy to let me come in. Maybe he didn't have a lot of friends. The only problem was that Danny's parents were out, and that left us with Danny's grandpa. And once he'd gotten started, Grandpa didn't seem to want to stop talking.

"They get you alone," he said, "where no one can see. They don't even want another crizzle around when that special time comes. It's the way they are—very private. And then they change, like a candle dripping. The skin melts off and there's the crizzle, all mean and hungry. There's nothing nastier in the whole wide world. It's not a pretty thing. And if you see a crizzle, that's the last thing you'll see, let me tell ya, the last thing you'll see." He stretched forward in his chair and shouted, *"Chomp!"*

I jumped.

He started laughing.

"Very funny," I said, trying not to act embarrassed. I hadn't been scared, just startled. "Thanks for the fascinating story."

"Anyone want to go for a walk in the woods?" Grandpa asked.

"No thanks," I said.

He got up and shuffled to the window. "Beautiful night," he said. "Lovely night for a walk." He turned and stared at me. "Come on, young man. How about a little stroll?"

"No, thank you," I said. "It sounds absolutely wonderful, but I'm not sure I could handle the excitement." There was something hungry in the old man's eyes. I'd never admit that his silly story had spooked me, but there was no way I was going to go anywhere alone with him right now.

He took his hat and coat from a hook on the wall, then spoke to Danny. "Beautiful night, isn't it?"

"Yes, Grandpa," Danny said.

Danny's grandpa opened the door and gazed outside. "Ah, smell that night air. Nothing like a good long walk. Really helps build up an appetite." Again, he stared at me. "Are you *sure* you don't want to go for a walk?"

"Maybe some other time."

"Suit yourself, but you don't know what you're missing." He stepped outside and closed the door. It shut with a clunk that shot through the room.

"Wow," I said, turning to Danny. "No offense, but your grandpa is kind of spooky. I could swear he was trying to get me alone."

Danny shook his head. "Nah, he wouldn't do that."

"How do you know?" I asked.

"He was just teasing," Danny told me. "He knew you wouldn't go with him."

I nodded. "You got that right."

"Besides, we take turns," Danny said. "Grandpa's real fair about that. And tonight, it's my turn." He grinned and winked at me.

"What?" I still didn't understand.

"Alone at last," Danny said. He started laughing. The grin spread wider as it dripped down his chin like stretched taffy.

I moved away until I felt the wall press against my back.

"Alone," he repeated. "Alone with a crizzle. Only one way that can turn out." Danny kept laughing as the flesh melted from his face like wax on a candle. And his eyes, even as they slid away to reveal what lay beneath, looked hungry. *Very* hungry.

LIGHT AS A FEATHER, STIFF AS A BOARD

They'd been playing the game all summer, and it had sort of worked, but Sharon suspected they hadn't really done it right. Each evening kids from around the neighborhood would gather on one of the lawns, and they'd select a victim. Sharon believed it had to be someone heavy. With a light kid like Ray or Julie, it wasn't much of a trick. But with a heavier kid, they'd know if the game was real.

The group wasn't exactly the same each night, but there were certain kids who usually came. And there were certain kids who usually messed everything up. Billy, for instance, would do almost anything to get a laugh, even if it meant ruining the game.

Sharon had spent most of the day playing with Julie. Now she noticed that several kids had gathered half a block away on Kate's front yard. "Come on," she said to Julie.

"I don't know," Julie said. "I don't think I want to play."

"Why not?" Sharon took a step away from her friend. She had to join the others before the game started. Once they formed the circle, it would be too late.

Julie wrapped her arms around herself as if trying to hold onto her decision. "Kate's so bossy. I hate that."

"I know how you feel," Sharon said. She looked down the street anxiously. The game would start any minute. "Just don't pay any attention to her. It'll be fun. And it's the last day of vacation. You can't miss it."

Julie shook her head. "I really don't want to go."

"Please," Sharon said. "It won't be as much fun without you."

"Oh, all right," Julie said. "If it means that much to you." They walked down the street and gathered with the rest of the kids. Behind them the last of the sunlight melted away in puddles of red and purple against the sky. It would be dark soon.

Up ahead, Sharon saw that Kate had already taken charge of the group.

"Let's do it," Kate said.

Anne stretched out on the ground and crossed her arms over her chest. She closed her eyes.

"No," Kate said, poking Anne's arm. "You're too light. Get up."

Anne stood without arguing, but Sharon could tell that the girl was disappointed.

Kate scanned the group like a shopper looking for the nicest piece of meat in the display case. "Hmmm, what about Todd?"

"Sure," Todd said, grinning at the honor. He took Anne's place on the ground.

"I knew your weight would come in handy someday," Billy said.

Everyone gathered around Todd. Sharon knelt by his left leg. She could feel a change in the air as the kids grew serious.

Kate, kneeling by Todd's head, started the game.

"Light as a feather, stiff as a board," Kate said.

In a circle, starting at Kate's left, each of the others repeated the phrase: "Light as a feather, stiff as a board."

Sharon spoke when her turn came, making sure she sounded properly serious and somber. Each of the remaining kids took a turn, ending with Ray.

"Todd was in a car accident," Kate said as she sent the next phrase around the circle.

Again, they each repeated the words.

As Sharon took her turn, she heard Billy snicker.

When his turn came, Billy said, "Todd wet his pants."

It wasn't that funny, but Sharon giggled along with some of the other kids. Even Todd started laughing.

"That does it!" Kate shouted. She stood up and glared around the circle. Sharon looked away, feeling angry with herself for laughing and ruining the game.

"This is the last day of vacation," Kate said. "We get messed up every time. I want to do this right just once. You kids always ruin it. You," she said, pointing at Billy. "Out! You"—she pointed at Nora—"out! And you, too."

Sharon found herself staring at Kate's finger, hovering like a dagger just inches from her face. "But . . ."

"Out!" Kate screamed.

Sharon got up and backed away from the circle. It was a stupid game, anyway, she told herself. It never worked right. After chanting all the phrases, you were supposed to be able to lift the "victim" in the center with just two fingers. The victim was supposed to rise into the air. But there were so many kids playing that it was no big trick. It wasn't like the person really floated.

Julie started to get up to join Sharon. "Stay," Kate ordered. "We need you."

Julie stood, her eyes shifting back and forth between Sharon and Kate.

"We don't have enough," Kate said. "You'll ruin everything if you go. It will be all your fault."

"Go ahead," Sharon said to Julie.

"You sure?"

"Yeah."

Julie shrugged and rejoined the others on the ground.

"Light as a feather, stiff as a board," Kate began. The chant went around the circle. Sharon watched, part of her hoping that someone would mess up but part of her wanting to see the game done perfectly just one time. She wasn't a member of the circle, but the chance to see it happen would still be special. She realized she'd lied to herself before—it wasn't just a stupid game. It was more than that. If it was done absolutely perfectly right, Sharon believed something wonderful would happen.

"Todd was in a car accident."

The chant made its path around the circle.

"Light as a feather, stiff as a board."

Perfect.

"Todd is in the hospital," Kate said.

Around it went.

"Light as a feather, stiff as a board."

As always in the game, the victim's condition grew worse with each turn.

"Todd is in a coma," Kate said.

It went around with no mistakes.

"Light as a feather, stiff as a board."

"Todd is dead," Kate said.

Each person in the circle repeated the phrase, quietly and seriously. The jokers were gone. Nobody seemed to want to ruin the magic this time. In the air that surrounded her, Sharon felt as if the night was listening, watching, waiting.

"Light as a feather, stiff as a board," Kate said.

The words took their path.

"Todd is in his coffin," Kate said.

The chant went around.

Kate started the last turn. "Light as a feather,

stiff as a board." Her voice trembled slightly on the final word, but she spoke it clearly.

Sharon held her breath, wondering if the phrase would reach the end without error.

It did. For a moment, everyone in the circle remained still, as if they couldn't believe they'd succeeded. Then, all together, the group stood. Holding two fingers of each hand beneath Todd, they raised their hands. Light as a feather, Todd rose. They lifted their hands to shoulder height. Then they raised their hands above their heads, supporting Todd on their extended fingers. Finally, when they reached the limits that their bodies could stretch, they stopped.

But Todd didn't stop.

At first Sharon thought it was a trick of the moonlight. But Todd floated slowly above the outstretched arms.

"It worked," someone gasped.

"Stop him," Sharon shouted. She ran through the circle of kids and leaped to catch hold of Todd. Her fingers brushed the back of his shirt, but he was too high for her to grab.

"Do something," Anne said.

Kate stood, staring up at Todd. "Stop that," she demanded. "Come down right now."

Todd continued to rise.

Sharon had an idea. "Do the whole thing backward," she said. "That might bring him down."

"I'll do it," Kate said as she pushed Sharon aside and knelt. "Quickly," she said. The others from the original circle joined her on the ground. Kate paused, moving her lips as if she was having a hard time working out the words. Finally, she said, "Board a as stiff, feather a as light."

"No, it all has to be backward," Sharon said.

Kate glared at her. "I just said it backward. Don't you know anything?"

"But it isn't all backward," Sharon said. "You still went first. You have to go last. And you have to go in the other direction and start with the last phrase."

"That makes sense," Julie said.

"Get out!" Kate yelled, pointing at Julie. "And you be quiet," she said, glaring at Sharon again.

Julie stood and joined Sharon. "It won't work," Sharon whispered to her. "I know it won't."

"Anyone else have anything to say?" Kate asked.

Nobody spoke.

"Board a as stiff, feather a as light," Kate said.

Sharon looked up. Todd was a dark splotch above her head. She hoped he would come down as slowly as he rose. But she was afraid it wouldn't work—not the way Kate was doing it.

"Accident car a in was Todd," Kate said, struggling to reverse each phrase.

But they were doing it without a mistake.

"Board a as stiff, feather a as light,"

Perfectly . . .

"Dead is Todd."

No mistakes . . .

"Board a as stiff, feather a as light."

Sharon fought the urge to shout, to stop them. "This is very wrong," she whispered to Julie.

Julie nodded. She seemed to know, too.

"Hospital the in is Todd."

"Board a as stiff, feather a as light."

"Coma a in is Todd."

"Board a as stiff, feather a as light."

"Coffin his in is Todd."

"Board a as stiff, feather a as light," Kate said for the very last time.

Each in the circle repeated the phrase.

They were done. Sharon raised her eyes to the night sky. Todd was now barely a smudged dot far over their heads, one dark star among all the bright ones. Sharon couldn't tell whether he was still rising.

"Is he coming down?" she asked Julie.

Julie didn't answer. Sharon felt a hand clutch her shoulder, fingers digging painfully into her skin. "Hey, that hurts," she said as she jerked away.

Julie was pointing with her other hand and making sounds that weren't quite words.

Sharon looked to where Julie pointed. She, too, froze. The kids in the circle were still kneeling. But they were no longer on the ground. The whole group was rising. They rose silently, each one staring straight ahead as if locked in place.

Finally, Julie spoke. "They should have done it your way," she said.

"I guess so." Sharon watched as Kate and the others rose. She couldn't even see Todd anymore.

"Should we try to bring them down?" Julie asked.

Sharon shivered as the night grew cooler. She really didn't want all those kids to float away like chimney smoke. "If we do the game wrong, who knows what might happen to us?"

"Yeah," Julie said. "We could just float away, too."

Sharon nodded. "That's not all—think what will happen if we do it right."

"What?" Julie asked.

Sharon took one last look at the rising circle. "We'll get Kate back. And that would be even worse."

THE EVIL TREE

▼

ne day, as Patrick was walking home from school, he noticed a tree with a door in its side. He'd walked past this same tree many times, but there had never been a door before. A man stood next to the tree. He looked like a soldier, but he wasn't wearing a uniform. He wore black pants and a black shirt with black buttons. The only color in his outfit was a gold buckle on his belt in the shape of a shield. His black hair was cut short. The man stood straight and stiff, but his eyes scanned slowly back and forth as if he was waiting for someone.

"What's this?" Patrick asked, pointing to the door. It looked like a small version of a castle door. It was built with planks of wood. That was the only part that made sense to Patrick—if a tree had a door, the door should be made of wood. The planks were braced with crossbars of iron. There were large hinges on the left side and a heavy bolt on the right.

The man didn't say anything.

"What is this?" Patrick asked again.

"You don't want to know," the man said.

"Yes, I do," Patrick said. He took a step backward, remembering that he wasn't supposed to talk to strangers.

"I really shouldn't tell you." The man turned his head away, as if pretending that Patrick didn't exist.

"Tell me," Patrick demanded. "Or . . ." He paused, trying to find the perfect threat. Sometimes he had to shout, sometimes he had to beg, and sometimes he had to whine. Sometimes he even had to pretend to be nice. But he always found a way to get whatever he desired. A ripple of excitement raced through Patrick as he thought of the perfect words. "Tell me or I'll scream that you tried to kidnap me."

"Would you really do something so nasty?" the man asked, still facing away from Patrick.

"Do you want to find out?" Patrick almost hoped he'd have a chance to start shouting.

The man sighed and turned back toward Patrick. "Very well. I'll tell you. But you must promise not to reveal my secret to anyone. Do you swear?"

"I swear," Patrick said. That was no problem. He'd grown very good at making promises, even when he had no intention of keeping them.

The man leaned forward and whispered. Patrick

strained to hear. "Evil," the man said. "This is where evil is stored to keep it away from the innocent people of the world."

"You're crazy." Patrick enjoyed the chance to be rude to this stranger.

"Perhaps," the man said. "But I am one of the guardians who have been given the task of protecting the world from evil."

"Yeah, right." Patrick was nearly certain that the man was crazy. But he couldn't walk away without finding out for sure. If the man was telling the truth, there could be something fabulous inside the tree. Patrick wondered what evil looked like—did it have claws or wings? Did it have snakes for hair? He wasn't afraid of such things—he was attracted to them. He had to see what was behind the door.

There was no reason to ask. It would be easier to just *take* what he wanted.

Patrick dashed forward and grabbed the bolt. He slid it free, then yanked hard. The door opened so fast Patrick almost lost his balance. He held onto the bolt and steadied himself, eager to see the evil.

There was nothing inside the tree.

"Hey, it's empty," Patrick said. He felt his jaws tighten as he gritted his teeth. It was all just some kind of stupid joke. The man would pay for tricking him. "You liar!" he screamed. "You stinking liar! This doesn't hold any evil!" Patrick's mind raced to find the best way to get even with the man.

With surprising suddenness and strength, the

man pushed Patrick. He lost his grip on the edge of the door and stumbled inside the tree. "This doesn't hold any evil!" Patrick shouted again as the door slammed shut, sealing the chamber in darkness. From outside, he heard three words.

"Now it does."

There was a scraping sound as the bolt slid into place. Then Patrick heard quiet footsteps, fading, fading away.

KIDZILLA

▼

When I woke up this morning, I was a lizard. I realized something was wrong the moment I rolled out of bed. The frame of the bed broke under my weight. I jumped as the mattress crashed to the floor, but I jumped too high, cracking my head on the ceiling and cracking the ceiling with my head. At the same time, my tail lashed the wall, knocking a large hole next to the window and spreading a shower of plaster. That made me sneeze, and I blew another hole in the wall.

"Hey, what's going on up there?" Dad shouted from below.

"Nothing," I tried to say. But it came out *"Arrrrannnggg."* This situation definitely had possibilities.

"Just keep it down," Dad said.

I made my way into the hall, doing only a little damage to one side of the door frame. I wish I could say the same about the toilet, but it shattered under the force of my you-know-what. Personal hygiene proved to be a challenge. I discovered I could pick up my toothbrush if I clutched it between both claws. It took almost the whole tube to clean all my teeth, but at least when I was done my mouth felt minty fresh. You wouldn't believe how bad a lizard's mouth can taste first thing in the morning.

Breakfast time.

I was hungry enough to eat a house.

Mom was making pancakes. "Hi, hon," she said as I crashed my way into the kitchen and crushed down onto a chair. "Help yourself to juice." She slid a plate stacked with pancakes onto the table.

I looked at the fridge and at my claws. The juice just didn't seem worth the effort. Luckily, I was able to hook the pancakes without too much trouble. They tasted so good, I even licked my claws.

"Oops," Mom said, glancing up at the clock. "Better get moving. You don't want to be late for school."

"Yes, Mom," I said. It came out as a low growl, along with a stream of fire that shot across the kitchen and melted the garbage can. Oops.

I snagged my backpack with one claw and went through the door. The warm sunlight felt great on my scales. As soon as I crashed through the front gate, I learned that the sidewalk along the street was made of pretty thin concrete. The stuff just crumbled under my feet. It was like walking on Rice Krispies. Actually, it made a pretty neat sound.

I was having so much fun crunching the concrete that I was almost late for school. The bell was just ringing when I smashed through the narrow door.

Sitting at one of those tiny desks was out of the question, so I stood in the back of the room. When Mrs. Franzski came in, she just glanced over at me and said, "Oh, Bradley, I see you've found a new spot. Well, as long as you're comfortable."

She was very big on making sure we all had the proper "learning environment." She even let Danny Mitty sit on the floor sometimes.

I didn't raise my claw during class. I was pretty sure that if I said anything, I might be unable to avoid adding a stream of fire that would fry some of my classmates. While I wasn't exactly buddy-buddy with everyone, there weren't any kids who'd done anything bad enough to deserve being flamed.

After our reading lesson, we had gym class. We were doing our physical fitness tests today, so my size and strength came in pretty handy. I ran faster than ever before. Even though I had tiny arms, my powerful shoulders allowed me to do great at pushups. I did well at everything except sit-ups. Somehow, I just wasn't built for them.

The rest of the morning went fairly smoothly. Lunch, however, looked like it might be a problem. They always served these really small portions in the cafeteria. Here I was, starving, ravenous, monstrously hungry, and the lady behind the counter plops this tiny little scoop of chicken surprise on my plate. Sorry. Not enough. I reached over the counter and grabbed the whole pan. Let me tell you—I must have been starving. Even the chicken surprise looked good. And, compared to the normal taste inside a lizard's mouth, it wasn't all that bad, either.

Back in class, I wondered whether there was any point in paying attention. I mean, my future was pretty much not going to be changed by my ability or inability to name all the state capitals. The career options for giant lizards would be more along the lines of knocking down buildings or making tunnels through mountains. But I'd been a kid all my life and a lizard for just a day. Old habits are hard to break and old fears are very powerful. So I stayed in class.

As we were leaving the room at the end of the day, Mrs. Franzski called to me. "Bradley, you didn't seem to be with us today. I hope you can pay more attention tomorrow."

"Sure," I said, though it came out as a bit of a roar.

She smiled, then went back to grading papers.

I headed home, walking along the same trail of crumbled sidewalk. Mom was making dinner. Dad was still at work. I went up to my room and melted all my toy soldiers, one at a time, with little puffs of breath. I hadn't played with them in years, so it was no big deal if I ruined them.

Dinner went pretty much like breakfast. It was fried chicken, so Mom didn't make a fuss when I ate with my hands. Lucky thing she hadn't made meat loaf—or soup.

I slept really well. All that crushing and crashing must have tired me out. When I woke, I got out of bed carefully. But I realized I didn't have to be very cautious. I wasn't a lizard anymore. This morning, I was a robot. Good thing, too. We're having a math test today.

EVERYONE'S A WINNER

"**C**OME-UH, COME-UH, COME-UH! COME AND TRY YER LUCK." The shout of the barker rang over the thousand other noises filling the cotton-candy air of the traveling carnival. "You there; yeah, you," he called as he leaned forward and pointed at Derek. "Give it a try."

Derek paused. He knew he should have kept walking, but he couldn't ignore someone who was talking to him. It was a curse. He was too polite. "No thanks," he said, a half smile nervously spreading across his lips.

"Everyone's a winner," the barker said. "Come on, what are you afraid of? I won't bite you."

Derek shrugged. What was he afraid of? It was only a game. Just skee ball, as a matter of fact. It looked easy enough to beat the score—250 points for a small prize, 300 for a medium, and a tough 420 for a large. Heck, Derek was sure he could hit 250 standing backward and tossing with his left hand. He dug in his pocket past the crumpled ride tickets and gum wrappers until his fingers found a quarter.

"That's the way," the barker said. "You can't win if you don't play."

Derek dropped the quarter in the slot. It hung for a second before being swallowed by the machine. There was a clunk, followed by the rumble of the nine balls rolling down toward Derek. He began to play. Derek winced as he got off to a bad start. The first shot was pretty poor. He took a breath and looked around. Nobody was paying the slightest attention to him. He rolled another lousy shot into the ten-point hole. Then he hit a thirty.

"Guess I needed to warm up," he said, half to himself and half to the barker. His next couple of rolls weren't bad. He hit a thirty and two forties, then rolled three balls in a row perfectly for fifties.

Twenty more, Derek thought, holding the last ball in his hand. He was at 280, more than enough for a small prize, but he knew it would be junk. An easy twenty points and he'd move up from totally worthless junk to worthless junk, or maybe even just plain old junk. *Nice and easy,* Derek thought as he swung the ball.

"COME-UH, COME-UH!"

Startled by the shout, Derek jerked his hand forward. The ball shot from his grip, bounced toward the targets, and plopped into the ten-point hole.

"A WINNER!" The man handed him a piece of green plastic. "Two-ninety. Small prize. Congratulations, kid. You're a real champ."

Derek turned the piece of plastic over in his hand and stared at it. "What's this?"

"A bracelet. You can trade up for more prizes. Play again?"

Derek was about to answer when he was shoved aside. "I'll try." A kid—a big, ugly, mean-looking kid—barged in front of Derek and jammed a quarter in the slot with a grubby hand.

"Everyone's a winner," the barker said, smiling. "And you're just in time for our scoring special." He reached up and flipped over the sign that displayed the prize scores.

"But—" Derek stepped back. He couldn't believe it—only 150 points for a small prize, and 200 for a medium. *Forget it,* he told himself. *There's always a trick. They never let you win anything good.* He stepped back another pace but kept watching. The kid stunk. He rolled mostly twenties, with a couple of lucky thirties. He ended up with 200 points.

"We have a winner!" The barker handed the kid a small stuffed animal.

Derek shook his head. Some people had all the luck. There was no way he was going to wait around for another turn if he had to watch this kid win prizes. He decided to ride the Spin-a-Thon again. That was more his speed. It was scary—not because the ride was so rough, but because all the equipment in the carnival looked like it was within half an inch of breaking down. Every time he took a seat on that rusty old ride, Derek couldn't help imagining the door flying open—or maybe the whole car just breaking off the shaft and hurtling through the air, carrying Derek like some medieval catapult boulder, rolling and tumbling as the crowd below screamed in panic. Yeah, the Spin-a-Thon sounded good.

The ride, as always, was uneventful. When Derek got off, he found himself walking past the skee ball booth again. The kid was still there. He was playing furiously, throwing ball after ball without pausing between shots. His shirt was soaked from the effort. Sweat dripped from his hair at the back of his neck. Sweat flew when he shook his head after each throw. A pile of stuffed animals lay at his feet.

Derek stopped to watch. "WINNER!" the barker shouted. "Medium prize," he said. He handed the kid another stuffed animal. "Medium also wins a free play." He reached down and pressed a button.

Derek heard the balls rolling out. *Darn,* he thought. *That could have been me.* If the kid got a free play each time he hit 200, he'd be playing forever. Derek would have loved another chance—especially with those easy scores. He knew he could hit 200 points. But the kid wasn't going to move. He was just going to stand there and win all the prizes.

Derek looked around for something else to do. There was a wagon set back a bit past the skee ball. A large sign in faded letters proclaimed BOBO, THE MAN-EATING MONSTER!!!

Derek knew it would be a rip-off. It would be a guy in a gorilla suit, or a mechanical dummy covered with fur, or some other kind of trick. But he was getting bored, and admission probably only cost half a buck. Derek was willing to waste a couple of quarters. He walked up the ramp to the front of the wagon. There was nobody at the ticket window.

"Hello?" Derek tried to look past the bars. "Hello? Anybody here?" He waited a moment, then moved to the door that was next to the window. He was about to call again when he heard people arguing inside the wagon.

"He has to be fed," the first voice said. It was a woman speaking.

"We fed him last week," a man said. "It's too soon. We can't have a pattern."

"Look, Charlie is already setting it up. Didn't you see him flip the sign? Besides, nobody ever remembers. Bobo will see to that."

"I wish I knew how Bobo did that," the man said. "I still can't believe the way the crowd forgets everything."

"It's not important how he does it," the woman said. "What matters is if he doesn't get fed, he might decide to change our deal. I wouldn't want him thinking about us as dinner."

"Okay," the man said, "I guess you're right. Let him loose."

"Bobo," the woman called. "Dinner time." There

was a rattling of chains, then a screech of animal joy.

Derek had heard enough. He started to back away from the door and down the ramp. He stumbled, tripping over the edge of a plank. Derek twisted his body as he fell, landing hard on his side.

"What was that?" he heard the woman ask.

"Doesn't matter right now," the man said. "Go get it, Bobo."

Derek felt the ramp shake, *thump-clunk, thump-clunk*. Something big was coming out. Something large and mean and hungry. He jumped up. A sharp pain shot through his ankle, nearly dropping him again. Behind him, a huge creature was squeezing through the door. Derek saw brown, leathery hide with patches of black fur. A smell like dead meat wafted over him. He almost threw up.

People in the crowd were looking at the trailer. Some of them ran. Others just kept staring. Then Bobo burst out and everyone was running and screaming.

Derek tried to run, but the pain searing through his ankle was so bad he almost passed out. Behind him, Bobo stood erect. He was as tall as the wagon. Bobo, like some nightmare cross between an ape and a lizard, was coming after him.

Derek hobbled away from the trailer. Ahead, he saw the skee ball game. In the middle of all the panic, two people weren't running. The kid was bending down to scoop up his stuffed animals. The barker was leaning against the side of the booth as if nothing special was happening.

The pain in Derek's ankle felt worse than anything he could ever have imagined—worse than the time he hit the curb with his bike and flew off, sliding across the sidewalk on both knees. Worse than the time he'd slammed his finger in the car door. But the thought of being Bobo's dinner was far worse than the pain that shot through his ankle. He pushed himself as much as he could without passing out.

Derek glanced back at the wagon. Bobo had clumped down to the bottom of the ramp. The creature shot a hungry look to either side, then stared straight at Derek. Bobo lurched toward him. Derek gritted his teeth and forced himself to go faster.

The kid, the one with all the stuffed animals, was right in Derek's path. Derek tried to go around. The kid was still fumbling with the animals. He dropped one. Derek hobbled past him, fire running up his leg and exploding in his brain.

He took several agonizing steps, then looked back. The kid straightened up, but a couple of the stuffed animals fell from his arms. He bent down and grabbed one of his prizes. A few more tumbled out of his grip. He'd won more prizes than he could possibly hold.

"Run!" Derek shouted at him.

The kid raised his head briefly, his face blank and empty, then looked back at the ground and tried to gather more of his winnings. Bobo was right behind him. The carnival beast raised a claw and swiped. Stuffed animals flew in a shower.

Everything slowed down for Derek, as if he was

watching someone else's dream. A soft object struck his chest. He clutched at it. A woman was behind Bobo. She said several words to the barker. It might have been, "Good job, Charlie."

"This one will hold him for a while," Charlie might have said. "Atta boy, Bobo. Take him inside. Good Bobo."

Around Derek, the crowd stopped running and screaming. The people stood for a moment, then shrugged or shook their heads and went back to their rides and games and food. After a while, Derek couldn't even remember what everyone had been so excited about.

"How was the carnival?" Derek's mom asked when he got home.

"Not bad." He limped into the living room.

"Did you hurt yourself?"

Hurt myself? Derek realized he must have twisted his ankle coming up the stairs. "I'm okay."

"Did you win that?" his mom asked.

Derek looked at the stuffed animal he was gripping. "Yeah, I guess so."

"They sure are giving away ugly prizes," his mom said.

Derek examined the animal. It was such a piece of junk, he couldn't even tell what it was supposed to be. Maybe it was a gorilla. It might even have been a lizard. It certainly didn't look like anything he'd ever seen before. *Well,* he thought as he carried his prize up to his room, *at least I won something.*

A LITTLE OFF
THE TOP

▼

Ryan checked his pocket to make sure he hadn't lost the money his mother had given him. It was still there. He hesitated at the door of the barbershop, wondering whether he could come up with any good excuse for skipping the whole unpleasant experience. Nothing came to mind. Best just to get it over with, he thought as he stepped inside. Life would be a lot easier if hair didn't grow so quickly. Ryan didn't like any part of going to the barbershop. He didn't like waiting for his turn, and he didn't like sitting in the chair, and he didn't like having his head moved and turned and twisted as Mr. Garafolo snipped at his hair.

"I'm here for my usual," Ryan said.

Mr. Garafolo turned toward Ryan. But it wasn't Mr. Garafolo—it was a different man. He was dressed the same, with the white shirt and black pants, and he held a pair of scissors in his hand, but he was not Mr. Garafolo. The barber rotated the empty chair toward Ryan. "Step right up."

"Uh, where's Mr. Garafolo?" Ryan asked.

"Tony's unavailable," the man said. "I'm his cousin, Vince Sweeny. Come on, you'll like the way I cut hair. You'll leave here with a big smile. You'll be grinning from ear to ear. I promise."

Ryan noticed there were no other customers in the shop. He wondered if this barber had scared them off by giving someone a bad haircut. "Maybe I should come back later . . ."

"No, no. Come on. Tony would want it this way," Mr. Sweeny said, pointing to the chair with his scissors. "Please."

"Okay," Ryan said. He noticed the way the hair clippings scattered in the breeze his feet made as they clomped on the old linoleum. It almost seemed as if the clippings were running from him.

Ryan climbed into the chair. The barber draped a large cloth over him and tied it around his neck. Ryan didn't know why barbers bothered with that sheet—the hairs always managed to sneak through and make him itch for hours after getting a cut.

"Now," the barber said, "how would you like it? Short? Medium? Are you one of those kids with the short top and long sides? You tell me."

"Short is good," Ryan said. He looked down at the cloth. There was a stain. It was dark red, almost brown. He stared at the splotch, wondering if it was blood.

Suddenly, hands grabbed his head and bent it back.

"Ah, that's better," the barber said. "Keep your head nice and straight. You don't want to wiggle around."

"Sorry," Ryan said.

The barber started snipping away at Ryan's head. Bits of hair went flying. Bits of hair, somehow, got through the collar. The barber pushed Ryan's head forward. Ryan raised his eyes and looked into the mirror. There was a door at the back of the shop, leading to a storage room. In the reflection of the rear wall, a foot stuck out on the floor by the door. *A foot?* Ryan started to turn his head.

"Sit still," the barber said, clamping his hands on Ryan's head and twisting it away from the mirror. "Keep still. I wouldn't want to cut you." The hand held hard and firm for a moment, then let go. "That's a good boy."

Ryan swallowed, trying not to move his head at all. *Who was this man?* Ryan realized he didn't know anything about the person who was standing behind him with the sharp, pointed scissors. He didn't even know for sure if the man was Mr. Garafolo's cousin, or if he was a real barber. He glanced at the cash register. The drawer was half open.

Maybe the man wasn't a barber at all.

Shifting his eyes far to the right, Ryan could just see the image in the mirror. For sure, it was a foot—there was a black shoe and the edge of a black pants cuff, like the black pants the barber wore. Like the black pants Mr. Garafolo wore.

The scissors moved close to his ear, making tiny snips. "Where did you say Mr. Garafolo was?" Ryan asked.

Snip!

Ryan jumped as the scissors took off a large hunk of hair right next to his ear.

"Easy, don't jump. You want to lose your ear?" The barber put his hand on Ryan's head again. He kept snipping, but he didn't answer Ryan's question.

Ryan clenched his fists under the sheet and closed his eyes.

"Relax," the barber said. "You'll be finished soon."

Ryan took a deep breath. It didn't help. There was no way he could relax, not with a body in the back room and this cold-blooded killer standing behind him.

"Just another snip, then a little touch-up with the razor," the barber said.

Razor? Ryan grabbed the arms of the chair and opened his eyes.

He flinched as the barber slapped shaving cream on the back of his neck. It felt warm and wet. Ryan could almost imagine that it was blood. He looked down at the splotch on the sheet again. There was a scritch-scratch sound as the barber sharpened the razor on the strop hanging from the chair.

From the corner of his eye, Ryan caught sight of motion in the mirror. The foot was twitching—he was sure of it. Then, from the room, he heard a scream, "Eeeeooowwwwerrr!"

Ryan ripped the sheet from his neck, jumped from the chair, and spun to face the barber.

"Hey, careful!" The barber threw his hand up, the razor gleaming as bits of lather flew into the air. "This thing is sharp. It could take your head right off."

Ryan tried to run but his feet tangled in the sheet. He hit the ground. There was another awful scream from the next room, "Eeeeoooowwwaaggghhh."

Lying on his side, tangled in the sheet, Ryan saw the foot move. It pulled back into the room. Ryan looked up. Mr. Garafolo stumbled out from the back room. Ryan expected to see him grab his throat and fall to the floor. But the barber was just stretching and yawning, making a sound like "Eeeeoooowwarrgleee."

Mr. Garafolo glanced at the empty chair. Then he stared at the floor. "Ryan. What's the matter? You don't like the way Vince cuts hair?"

"Uh . . ." Ryan untangled himself from the sheet, stood up, and plopped into the chair. "He does a great job."

"You're a nice boy, Ryan," Mr. Garafolo said, "but you are a little jumpy. Try to relax. You'll live longer." He turned to Vince and said, "Thanks for letting me take a nap. The doctor was right— my back feels a lot better when I sleep on a hard floor. You can go now. I'll finish Ryan."

Finish me? Ryan thought. He started to leap from the chair again.

"Calm down," Mr. Garafolo said, clamping a

hand on Ryan's shoulder. "This is supposed to be a pleasure."

Ryan tried not to flinch as the razor scraped across the back of his neck.

"Okay," Mr. Garafolo said a minute later. "All done."

Ryan paid Mr. Garafolo and walked out of the shop. "Come back soon," he heard Mr. Garafolo call as the door closed behind him.

Ryan took a deep breath. It felt great to be standing in the bright sun and fresh air.

What a perfect day, Ryan thought as he walked down the street. It would be a perfect and wonderful and stunningly great day, except for one small thing. Now that he was done with the barber, it was time for his appointment at the dentist. Running his hand through his hair and gritting his teeth, Ryan headed across town.

THE SLIDE

Kay plopped down on the bench at the edge of the playground and set Tommy loose. "Go play," she said as she took a can of soda out of her backpack. "Have fun. Don't get hurt." She watched him scurry off to the monkey bars. All around, she saw little kids having mindless fun, running and laughing and squealing like upright pigs.

"Unbelievable," Kay said to herself.

She had dragged Tommy all around town, then just picked a direction and started walking, hoping he would be exhausted enough to sleep most of the afternoon once she got him back to his house. If he slept, she'd be free to hang out and watch TV.

But she couldn't take him home for another hour. His mother had explained that she needed her *per-*

sonal time each morning. Kay had to keep Tommy out of the house until noon. It was part of her job.

Kay hated playgrounds, but she got paid the same cheap baby-sitting rate whether she read to the little creature or played with him or just set him loose to romp and frolic. She saw no point working herself ragged for a couple of dollars an hour.

Kay tried to remember if she'd visited this playground before. She'd been watching Tommy almost every day for these first three weeks of summer, and she'd dragged the sticky little nose-picker to a lot of places. They'd all looked pretty much the same. This one was a bit shabbier than some. But it wasn't like any of the equipment was actually dangerous. It wouldn't do to bring the little bug home with broken parts. Kay suspected Mrs. Walton wouldn't pay her if her precious Tommy snapped an arm or a leg or cut his fore-head open on a rusty piece of jagged metal.

There didn't seem to be any danger of that at the moment. The monkey bars looked safe enough to Kay. The little cockroach wasn't so high up that a fall would fracture anything important. Kay settled back on the bench and glanced around. Usually there were other sitters to talk to. Not today.

Next to the bench, Kay saw a garbage barrel, and next to that another large barrel for aluminum cans. A sign on the second barrel read: PLEASE RECYCLE. Kay sipped the last drops of her soda, then tossed the can toward the barrels. It hit the rim of one, then bounced to the ground. Kay laughed. It didn't matter if she missed—someone would pick it up. That was the nice thing about recycling, as far as Kay was concerned—there was always someone willing to step in and do the job.

No matter how unpleasant a job, there was always someone who would do it . . . for a price. Kay knew she was living proof of that theory. But there were lots of worse things in life than watching a slimy little grub run around. And it wasn't like she'd be doing it the rest of her life.

Kay looked at the piece of equipment nearest her bench. It was one of those tube slides—a big, slanted plastic tube with a ladder at one end. The middle of the tube was held up from the ground on another short tube. A little kid was just springing out the bottom. Kay watched him slide to the ground and land on his feet. His untied sneakers hit the dirt with a *plock*. He bent his knees, taking the jolt like an expert, and ran off. A moment later, a second kid came out. *Plock.* Kay glanced at the top—there were no other kids waiting to enter the slide.

For a moment, Kay thought about going through the slide herself. It almost looked like fun. But she was too old for that. And what if one of her friends saw her? She'd never live it down.

"Kay! Watch me!" Tommy screamed from the monkey bars. He was hanging from a bar at one corner, swinging his body and kicking his legs. Kay turned her head his way for a moment. She didn't even bother trying to appear interested. The little worm seemed satisfied just to have her eyes aimed in his direction.

Plock. Another kid had just come out of the

tube slide. Like the first two, he hit the ground with both feet and went running off.

Kay hadn't noticed him at the top of the ladder. She realized the kid must have climbed in when she'd looked toward Tommy. For all the noise they usually made, there were times when little kids could move as silently as spiders.

"Push me, Kay!" Tommy called as he ran from the monkey bars to the swings. "Push me! Push me! Push me! Push me!"

"They don't pay me enough for this," Kay muttered as she trudged over to him. She noticed that there were a lot of kids in the playground. They all looked the same, except for Tommy, who was a stupid little four-year-old dressed in jeans and a red shirt. The rest of them were mostly stupid little four-year-olds dressed in jeans and blue shirts.

Kay gave Tommy a push, resisting the urge to shove the ridiculous creature right off the swing, then went back to the bench. As she sat, another kid came out of the slide. He hit—*plock*—stood for a second as if figuring out where he was, then went running off to the seesaws.

Kay could have sworn she hadn't seen anyone go in the top. She got up and walked to the slide, then bent to look inside the bottom of the tube. An odd smell drifted out, moist and old, like the scent of earth beneath a rock. Kay could barely make out a dark place where the slide rested on the support tube. It almost looked like a hole, but she knew that couldn't be right. If there were a hole in the middle, the kids would fall in.

Unless . . .

Kay had a glimmer of an idea, but it was too strange. She let it go and went back to the bench. Tommy came running over. "Play seesaw with me," he demanded.

Kay shook her head. The last thing she wanted was a seat full of splinters. "Why don't you make some friends?" she suggested.

"They don't like me," Tommy said.

Now there's a surprise, Kay thought. But all she said was, "Go back to the swings. Practice pumping. I'll be right here."

Tommy ran off. Kay watched as he wove his way around the other kids, keeping as much distance from each of them as possible. It reminded her of a video game.

A moment later, another kid came sliding out of the end of the tube. *Plock.* The place was crawling with kids. Kay was sure it was more crowded now. There were kids piled on the seesaws and the swings and all over the climbing equipment. There were kids running around chasing each other in a nonstop game of tag. But there weren't any parents or sitters in sight. Kay glanced at the parking lot next to the playground. It was empty. She thought about leaving. Tommy would pitch a fit. But he'd do that whether they left now, or in ten minutes, or in ten hours.

Kay checked her watch. It was only a few minutes after eleven. She figured she'd wait another half hour, then drag Tommy home. With luck, he'd be tired by then.

As Kay sat and waited for time to pass, she noticed something odd. There weren't any girls in the playground. Kay looked around to make sure she wasn't mistaken. As she did, another little kid popped out from the end of the tube slide. It was a boy. He looked just like all the others.

It was almost as if— No, she dropped that thought. It was too ridiculous.

"Don't be silly," she whispered. Kay shifted uncomfortably on the bench. Maybe it was time to leave.

Another kid came out of the slide.

Maybe it was time to leave *right now*.

Yes. Time to get Tommy and head home, Kay thought. It was definitely time to get out.

Plock. Two more feet hit the dirt in front of the slide.

Kay jumped up from the bench. The playground was swarming with kids. They were everywhere. Everywhere except the top of the slide, Kay realized. She was certain she hadn't seen a single one of those kids go in the top.

They all just slid out the bottom.

It was almost like . . . She took a deep breath, not wanting to think about that image but unable to keep her mind from turning down that dark corner—*almost like insects*. Kay shivered as she remembered a film she'd seen in science class. In a disgustingly large close-up shot, a swollen termite queen was popping out one egg after another. Smooth, slimy, white eggs squeezed out. *Plock*. Thousands of them. *Plock, plock, plock*. Kay couldn't wipe the image from her mind. She knew what was happening. Instead of eggs, the tube was plocking out snotty little kids, creating thousands of workers to serve its needs.

"That's crazy," Kay said.

She started to move away from the bench.

"Kay, look at me!" Tommy shouted from high up on the swings.

Kay hesitated. She wanted to run from the playground, but there'd be big trouble if she left Tommy. She stepped toward him.

Kids swarmed forward and blocked her way. Another kid slid from the slide. *Plock*—his feet hit the dirt. The mob moved closer. They were all around her. Except for the swing that held Tommy, the equipment was empty. They'd all left the swings and seesaws and monkey bars to gather around her. Kay could feel them pushing in from the sides and from behind.

Insects, Kay thought as she stared into the empty faces of little kids closing in around her. They pressed closer. They all looked the same, and none of them looked quite right. This close, Kay saw that their arms were a bit too long, their heads a bit too small. The skin of their fingers as they grasped at her was slippery and wet.

Plock. Another kid came from the slide. *Plock. Plock.* Two more.

Kay was sure, now.

They surged against her. They shoved. They herded. They lifted her. Kay grabbed the bench, struggling to keep her feet on the ground. They pried her fingers loose and raised her over their heads. Dozens of hands held her up in the air.

"No!" Kay screamed.

They carried her toward the slide.

"Not there!" Kay tried to twist from their grip. "Please, not there . . ."

None of the kids spoke. But all together, they produced a droning buzz that filled her ears.

Across the playground, Tommy was still swinging, trying to pump himself higher.

Little rat, Kay thought. *No,* she realized. He wasn't a rat. He was an insect. They were all insects.

They hauled her toward the top of the slide. Behind her, more were born. *Plock. Plock. Plock.* They lifted her higher, crawling on top of each other to form a mound. The droning buzz grew louder and louder until it filled her head and made her body vibrate. The tube swallowed the sunlight as Kay slid in. She clutched at the edge for an instant, but a dozen tiny hands pushed her deeper.

Kay lost her grip. She slid. Halfway down, she fell into a hole. For an instant, Kay remembered the high dive, and the stomach-lurching feeling of plummeting toward the water.

Kay dropped.

Her fall ended far too soon. She hit something large and soft and moist, like a giant, living wound. Kay sank. Ankles, knees, then thighs slipped into the goo. It was a huge insect, Kay realized, living in darkness, too swollen to move, buried in a hive beneath the playground, producing countless insect children. Here it waited, fat and slow and blind.

Beneath her, in a voice that came right into her

mind, she heard a huge and old and terribly strange life-form speak.

"*Oh, good,*" it said. "*You are here. Good. Thank you, my children.*"

Kay sank deeper into the moist mass of flesh. All around, she could feel the little ones emerging, scrambling out and climbing toward the tube that led to the middle of the slide.

Kay's last thought almost made her laugh. This creature was about to absorb her, using her to create more of its own kind. She realized she was about to be recycled.

Somewhere outside and above, the buzz of the children drowned out any sounds Kay made.

BIG KIDS

▼

My friend Stu is scared of just about everything. He's almost a year younger than me. I guess that makes a difference, because he's always saying "Watch out for this," or "Look out for that." He's especially scared of the Big Kids. He'll say, "Don't go in there, Danny, the Big Kids will get you," or, "We'd better leave before some Big Kids come."

I don't see what the problem is—I'll bet I could outrun any Big Kid. I could probably outfight most of them, too. Not that I want to find out . . .

We'd been swimming in the quarry that day. Actually, *I'd* been swimming. Stu was too chicken to go into the water. He was afraid he'd get a cramp and drown, or that some girls would come along and see him in his underwear. So I was swimming and Stu was sitting. That's when I got the idea. "Hey, Stu," I said, treading water.

"Yeah?" He glanced up from the stick he was peeling.

"It's too hot here. Let's go to the caves."

He stared at me like I had suggested we jump off a bridge. "No way. There might be Big Kids there."

"Come on, nobody goes there. It'll be great."

Stu shook his head. I got out of the water and climbed up the steep bank. In a few minutes, the hot sun had dried me better than any towel could. "Come on, the caves."

"No."

"Come on. Are you chicken? Let's go."

Stu shook his head. "I don't want to."

I put on my jeans and shirt. "I'm going. You do what you want." I'd learned that trick from my parents. I started walking. In a few seconds, I heard Stu running to catch up.

"But what if there are—"

"No problem. I'll deal with anything that comes up." After all this talk, I was almost hoping to run into some Big Kids. I'd show Stu there was nothing to worry about.

Stu jabbered a bit more on the way to the caves, but I didn't pay much attention. He hung back when I reached the entrance. I went ahead without waiting for him. It got dark pretty quickly, but there were enough cracks and openings that the passageways never got completely black. I figured Stu would catch up with me in a minute. I went a few feet farther, then stopped, expecting to hear

Stu chugging up behind me. Instead, I heard a shout.

"Ow!"

I ran back to the entrance. Wouldn't you know that bad stuff always happens to whoever expects it to happen? I think if you're afraid enough of something and worry enough, it almost has to happen. So there was Stu, caught by the one thing he feared the most. Yup, the Big Kids had him. They formed a ring around Stu and were pushing him back and forth, like a game of human hot potato. His face was pretty much frozen with terror and red enough to use for a stop sign.

I figured I could wait and see how bad it got, or I could rush in now and try to help him. So far, they were just pushing. There was a good chance they'd get bored with Stu and leave him in a minute or two.

I'd forgotten that Big Kids can get really cruel when they're bored.

One of them hit Stu a hard shot to the stomach. "Ooff," Stu grunted. He doubled over and staggered back, crashing into the Big Kid who was closest to the mouth of the cave.

I was moving before I even realized what was happening.

As the Big Kid stumbled from the impact, I stuck my foot out behind him. He went over backward. I reached out, grabbed Stu by the arm, and yanked.

"Huh?" he cried out.

"Shut up and run." I pushed Stu ahead of me.

The surprise was worth a few seconds' head start. There was a good chance we could escape.

"Get them!" one of the Big Kids shouted from behind us.

Stu was whimpering, but he kept up his speed. I herded him, taking the familiar turns. I really knew the caves as well as anyone.

At least, I thought I did.

After a while, the sound of the Big Kids' footsteps faded. We'd escaped. At worst, they'd be waiting at the mouth of the cave. But they wouldn't stay there forever. They'd get tired of waiting, and they'd leave.

"Thanks," Stu said quietly when we stopped running.

"Anytime."

"I told you the Big Kids would get us."

I nodded. But there were more important worries to distract me. I was pretty sure I knew the way out, but the chamber around us didn't seem familiar. I started tracing the way back, trying to remember the path we'd taken.

"You sure this is how we came?" Stu asked.

"I don't know." I didn't recognize the shaft we were in. It led up at a slight angle, but it kept getting narrower. The ceiling was so low, I was almost crawling.

"This can't be right," Stu said.

"Yeah. Maybe we should turn back." I looked ahead. "Hang on—I think it gets wider." Sure enough, a bit farther along the shaft got bigger. Then it opened into a large chamber.

And there were Big Kids there.

Different Big Kids.

I didn't see them at first. I climbed up on a boulder that was near the opening. It was warm. It moved. It wasn't a boulder. It was a toe. A big toe . . .

Stu made a gurgling sound as he stared at the huge foot. To be fair, I wasn't saying much either. In fact, I'm sure any bat in the cave would have had no trouble flying into my open mouth at that moment.

"Hi," one of the Big Kids said. His voice rumbled through the chamber. I looked up. Trickles of light filtered in from cracks in one of the side walls, but the speaker's head was lost in the darkness far above me.

"Uh . . . hi," I said.

"Whatcha doing?" another voice asked.

"We were running from some Big . . . uh, from some bullies," I told him.

"I hate bullies," the first Big Kid said.

"Me, too," another agreed.

"So do I."

I was surprised by this last voice. It was Stu. I guess once you face your worst fears, you can either crumple up or you can deal with things. To my surprise, Stu seemed to be dealing with the situation. "If you tell me how to get out of here," he said, "I'll bring some tiny little bullies for you to play with. Okay?"

"Deal," one of the Big Kids said. A huge hand descended from the darkness and reached out to seal the bargain with a shake. Stu held out his own insignificant, microscopic hand and grasped the Big Kid's fingertip.

"Go straight back until you reach the wall," the Big Kid said. "Then keep making lefts. You can't miss the exit."

"Thanks." Stu headed out.

I started to follow him, but he turned and said, "Stay here. This is for me to do."

He went off, walking tall, then ducked into the tunnel and disappeared. I stayed and made small talk with the Big Kids. I wasn't sure what they were like, and I didn't want to say anything that might upset them, so I let them do most of the talking. In a while, I heard the sounds of a mob heading this way. Stu came racing in, panting and puffing but looking pretty happy to be in the lead.

"Get the little weasel!" someone behind him shouted.

"Smash him!"

"Pound him to bits!"

They came tearing in after Stu, popping one by one through the narrow opening like marbles spilling out of a bottle.

Hands swept down and grabbed the bullies the way I'd grab a root beer from the cooler in the corner store. The hands rose again, with tiny arms and legs dangling at all angles, kicking and twitching and flailing. There were some shouts and a lot of whimpers.

"Thanks, guys," Stu said as we walked to the exit of the chamber.

"Our pleasure," a Big Kid said. He rattled a

bully in his fist like a can of spray paint that needed mixing. "Thanks for the toys. Come see us again."

"We sure will," Stu said. He led us out.

"What do you feel like doing?" I asked as we walked away from the mouth of the cave. It was still early.

"I don't know," Stu said.

"How about the dump?" I suggested.

Stu's face creased with a frown. "But there might be . . ." He stopped, and the frown faded. Then he smiled. "Sure," he said. "Let's go."

YOUR WORST NIGHTMARE

▼

It's over. The nightmare is over. Just in time. I couldn't run much farther. I could hardly breathe. Larry looked even worse. But we didn't have to run. I'd saved us. My idea worked. I could stand here now and catch my breath and wonder how things had gotten so quickly out of hand.

I probably shouldn't have been hanging out with Larry in the first place. He can be a really big jerk. But I'm not too good at making friends, so I didn't have a lot of choices. I usually ended up spending my free time with Larry. Mostly, I didn't get involved when he was being a jerk. I didn't try to stop him, but I didn't take part.

But the Clayton kid blamed both of us. It was all Larry's doing. That didn't matter. We both got blamed.

I don't know where Larry got the phrase—probably from some movie. That's how it started with the Clayton kid. What was his name? Ricky. That was it—Ricky Clayton. He's this real quiet kid who doesn't ever bother anyone or do anything much at all. Even so, there's something spooky about him.

But mostly I guess he was in the wrong place at the wrong time. He was walking down the street toward Larry when Larry was in that mean mood of his.

"Hey, what are you looking at?" Larry said as the kid got close to him.

"Nothing," the kid mumbled. I guess he didn't realize what a dangerous answer that was.

"Nothing? You calling me nothing?" That's when Larry grabbed the kid by the shirt. Larry really liked to do that. He'd grab a handful of cloth and buttons, right below the neck, and then twist his fist. I think he'd gotten that from a movie, too.

"Come on, leave me alone." The kid squirmed a bit but didn't try to break loose.

"You know what I am?" Larry asked him. I could tell he was getting ready to use the phrase.

The kid shook his head.

"You know what I am?" Larry yelled, putting his face right up close so his nose was almost in the kid's eye.

"No . . ."

"I'm your worst nightmare." Larry gave the kid a push.

The kid stumbled backward and fell down hard

on his butt. I expected him to start crying, or to turn and run. He wasn't very big. Larry would never do something like that to anyone who had a chance of fighting back. But the kid didn't cry or run. Instead he stared at Larry and said, "You don't know anything about nightmares."

I guess that took Larry by surprise. He didn't say a word. Then the kid spoke again. "But you will. Real soon." He stood up slowly, his eyes still locked on us. "Your worst nightmare is coming. It's on its way."

"You're crazy," Larry said. He shook his head. "Let's get out of here. This kid has lost his mind."

I didn't need much convincing. The Clayton kid was far too strange. We walked away. Behind us, I heard the kid say, "For both of you."

As we went down Lincoln Street, the breeze picked up. The air filled with whirling maple seeds that had been blown down from three trees that grew in the yard of a house near the corner.

Whenever I saw Larry rough up someone, I found myself acting extra friendly afterward, sort of wanting to make sure he still liked me. Maybe that's why I started to tell him my deep secret. "Hey, you ever pretend that those seeds are—"

"What was that?" Larry said, pointing in front of us.

I didn't see anything. "Where?"

He shook his head. "Nothing. Let's go this way." He turned down Spring Street.

"Sure." I followed and thought about spilling my secret. But Larry had other things to talk about.

"Did you see that kid's face when I pushed him?" he asked, grinning. He opened his eyes wide, imitating the kid, then snorted in amusement.

"Yeah, he really looked surprised," I said.

"*Bam*, right down on his butt," Larry said. "That'll teach him to show me some respect."

"You got that right," I said.

We'd gone less than a block when Larry stopped again. This time he just stood there and pointed.

This time, I saw it.

He must have been close to seven feet tall. He might have been alive once. Imagine a man made inside out. Give him claws. Give him fangs and an attitude. Now imagine something twice as awful. That's what stood in front of us. If he caught up with us, I think we'd get torn to pieces quicker than you could let out a scream. From the muscles that rippled on the outside of his arms, I know he could pull us apart as easily as a couple of wet napkins.

Larry turned and ran down Spring, crossing Lincoln. I stuck right with him.

"What was that?" I managed to ask as we ran.

"My nightmare," Larry told me. "My worst nightmare."

"Oh man. You dream that kind of stuff?"

Before Larry could answer, we had to stop. The monster from his nightmare was in front of us, at the corner of Spring and Hickory.

This time, he was closer.

Just like in a nightmare.

We cut down Spring Street. "Let's go to one of the houses," I said. "Let's get inside."

"No. I do that sometimes in the nightmare. Then I'm trapped."

"Do you ever get away?" I asked.

Larry shook his head. "He always catches me."

We ran. He chased us, but he always ended up ahead of us. "We're dead," Larry gasped. He was panting so hard he was spraying spit with each breath. "That kid. He did this."

I thought about the kid. As we'd left, he'd said, "For both of you." For Larry for what he'd done, and for me for standing there and letting it happen. The very thought of my worst nightmare coming to life made my guts churn. But maybe two bad things could cancel each other out.

"This way," I said, heading back toward Lincoln.

Larry followed. He was starting to moan softly each time he breathed. I think he was running out of strength. "Sometimes, I find a gun," Larry said, gasping between sentences. "I shoot it, but it keeps coming."

"This time is different," I said.

We made it to Lincoln. We had to keep changing direction on the way. But we made it. I stopped before we reached the maple trees. "We can rest here," I told Larry. "We're safe."

"What . . . ?" That was all Larry could get out.

"That's my worst nightmare," I said, looking at the trees.

"Huh?" Then Larry pointed toward the corner. "Got to run." His nightmare stood ahead of us, at the other side of the maples.

"No. Let him come."

I waited. I think Larry still wanted to run, but

he couldn't find the strength. I watched the seeds whirling down, imagining what would happen if they suddenly became as sharp as razors.

A stray seed whirled at me, caught by a gust of wind. The seed glanced off my forehead. I could feel something warm and wet running down my face. Blood. In front of us, Larry's nightmare slowly lurched forward. But it was almost over. Larry's worst nightmare was about to walk right through my own worst nightmare.

"We're okay," I said.

"You're bleeding."

I shook my head. "Doesn't matter." I held my breath for a moment as Larry's nightmare tried to pass through the cloud of swirling seeds. It was like watching tomatoes in a blender. I had to turn away. I looked at Larry's face. He was staring straight ahead, watching his nightmare get shredded.

"My nightmare . . ." He still hadn't caught his breath.

"It's okay," I said. "It's over."

"My nightmare," he said again. He kept staring. I didn't know how he could stand to look at that mess. "Sometimes, I find an ax." He took a small step backward.

"It's over," I said. I risked a peek beneath the maples. Larry's nightmare was now thousands of scattered shreds.

"I use the ax. I chop my nightmare to pieces." He took another step back. Then he grabbed my shirt and twisted it and put his face an inch from mine. "It doesn't matter. The pieces just keep coming."

I looked past Larry to the spot where his nightmare should have ended.

"No," I gasped as my blood froze in my veins and my muscles fell slack from fear. "No . . ."

Larry was right. The pieces were coming. They were small. But they were fast. Suddenly, the maple seeds didn't seem all that awful. Suddenly, I had a new worst nightmare. I tried to run, but the pieces were everywhere.

PHONE AHEAD

Normally, Joe wouldn't pick through garbage, but he'd glimpsed the edge of a shiny plastic case in the trash basket on the corner of Watson Street. *Electronics,* he thought as he leaned over and reached inside. Oh yes. Whatever it was, it certainly wasn't trash. *Who would throw out a cellular phone?* Joe wondered as he pulled the object from its nest of crumpled papers and crushed cans.

"Probably doesn't work," he said to himself as he flicked the on/off switch and held the phone to his ear. That's when he got his first surprise of the day. He heard someone talking. Joe listened for a moment, then said, "Hello? Hey, I found this phone. Can you hear me?"

But the voice on the other end didn't respond to

him. The man was speaking to someone else. "I just saw it on the news," the man said.

"Lucky everybody got out," a woman said. "Can you imagine what would have happened if there were lots of people in the bus station when the fire started? That would have been terrible."

The bus station? Joe thought. He hadn't heard anything about a fire, and he hadn't heard any sirens. But if the man just saw it on the news, it might still be happening. Joe had to go see. He switched off the phone and slipped it in his pocket. Then he jogged to the bus terminal.

"They must be crazy," he said when he reached the station. There was no sign of a fire. Joe looked at the clock on the bank across the street. It was seventy-four degrees. It was ten in the morning. He went home and put the phone in his desk drawer.

That evening, Joe was walking through the living room as his parents watched the news. "A fire broke out at the bus station around five this evening," the announcer reported.

Joe couldn't believe it. He listened to the rest of the story, trying to compare the details to what he had heard on the phone.

"No one was hurt, but the station was badly damaged. We'll have more information on the eleven o'clock report."

A shiver ran down Joe's back, then twisted through his stomach. He rushed to his room and grabbed the phone. He switched it on, but all he got was dead silence.

He tried the phone again an hour later. The line

was still dead. But on the next try, right before he went to bed, Joe heard the two people talking again.

"I just hate this weather," the man said.

Joe looked out the window. Stars twinkled in a cloudless sky.

"I don't mind the rain," the woman said, "but ever since I was a kid I hated thunder."

Joe could hear a crackle over the line like there was lightning in the air. *Definitely crazy,* he thought as he turned off the phone and went to sleep.

Six hours later, clouds filled the night sky. A heavy rain fell. The first thunderclap woke Joe. Lightning danced across the clouds in jagged flashes. *Maybe they aren't crazy,* Joe thought as he watched the storm.

Joe started checking the phone as often as he could. Whatever the man and woman talked about—the weather, the news, the latest episode of their favorite television show—happened just as they said. But each event took less time to come true than the last. The future Joe overheard in the phone kept getting closer to the present. But none of it was worth anything to him.

The next day, Joe finally heard something exciting.

"Imagine that," the man said. "All those bags of money lying there—right on Adams Street, just past the corner at Main."

"Can you believe it was there for over an hour before the police found it?" the woman asked. "The robbers must have dropped the loot when they were getting away. Good thing Adams isn't a busy street. It's still pretty amazing nobody picked up the money."

Joe switched off the phone. This was better than knowing the weather or the news. This was information he could use. Main and Adams streets were less than half a mile away. Joe started running. He reached Main and headed toward Adams. As he turned the corner, he saw bulging canvas bags scattered across one side of the street.

Joe ran down the block, his eyes fixed on the sacks. A police car came speeding past. It slid to a stop right next to the money. Two officers jumped out, grabbed the sacks, and tossed them into the trunk.

"Stupid phone," Joe said as he watched the patrol car drive away. He was so frustrated he almost threw it in the garbage. What good was knowing the future, he asked himself, if he couldn't get there in time?

Joe started walking home, holding the phone in his hand. He kept wondering what the man and woman were discussing right now. Probably chatting about the weather, he thought. Or something stupid, like a new movie. But maybe it was something *really* important . . .

Joe felt like he was holding onto the last piece of popcorn from a box. He couldn't leave it untasted. He had to try again. As he started across Bridge Street, he switched on the phone. *Tell me something I can use,* he thought. *That's all I want. Tell me something important. Just one small thing.*

He held the phone to his ear. They were talking. Joe relaxed. Hearing the voices was like running into old friends.

"Poor kid," the woman was saying.

There was a sadness in the woman's tone that caused Joe to stop walking and listen carefully.

"Yeah, I saw it on the news. It's a shame he died."

Joe shook his head. "Who cares," he muttered. This didn't sound like anything useful or important. But he kept the phone to his ear. He couldn't help himself.

"He was just standing there," the man said, "right in the middle of Bridge Street, by the place where the road curves. Imagine that. I wonder what was on his mind? They say he didn't even see the truck."

Truck? Joe thought as he heard the blare of a horn and the shriek of large tires skidding around the curve behind him. *What truck?*

"Cool," Lisa said as she looked down into the garbage can next to a lamppost on Bridge Street. She reached inside, wondering why someone would throw away a cellular phone. "Probably doesn't even work," she said. She switched it on and held it to her ear. She smiled as she heard voices. This, she thought, could be very interesting.

SAND SHARKS

Kelly had the sand castle almost perfect when Michael ran across the beach, screaming like a wild man. He smashed right through her marvelous castle, blowing it into fine fragments of sand that fell in a shower around her.

"Michael!"

"Sorry," he said, barely glancing over his shoulder. "Didn't see it."

"Yes you did. You ruined it on purpose."

Michael turned toward Kelly and shook his head. "Didn't," he said in a calm voice.

"Did!" Kelly shouted.

"Kids," Dad said, looking up from his magazine. "Stop fighting. This is supposed to be a vacation. Kelly, you're old enough to know how to behave. You should set an example for Michael."

"But Michael ruined my castle," Kelly said. "And he did it on purpose. Just like he ruins everything."

Mom glanced up from her book. "I'm sure it was an accident. There's no need for all this shouting." She shifted her eyes back to her reading before Kelly could answer.

Kelly looked at Michael. Michael looked back, grinning. Then, as if to make sure she knew it was no accident at all, he stuck out his tongue.

Kelly grabbed a fistful of sand, squeezing it so hard she could almost imagine it forming into a hunk of rock. It would feel wonderful to hurl it at Michael. That would knock a little manners into him. Her arm tensed.

"Listen, kids," Dad said, "your mom and I want to go back to the hotel and pick up some lunch for everyone. Can we trust the two of you to stay here alone?"

"Sure," Michael said. "No problem."

Kelly let the sand trickle from her fingers. *Alone out here?* The place was so bare and empty. They were the only people on the beach, and there weren't a whole lot of people on the island. A dozen frightening thoughts flashed through Kelly's mind.

"Well, Kell?" her Dad asked.

"Better take her with you," Michael said. "She's scared."

"Am not," Kelly said. She looked at her dad. "Sure, we'll be fine." The words fell from her mouth like specks of foam at the edge of a wave. In an instant, they were lost on the beach.

"Stay out of the water," Mom said. "We'll hurry back."

Kelly watched her parents walk up the beach to the road and wedge themselves into the small rental car. In a moment, the car was puttering along the narrow pathway. In another moment, it was out of sight.

Michael headed right for the ocean.

"Hey," Kelly said, "they told us not to."

"They aren't here, are they?" Michael walked deeper, kicking up water with each step.

Kelly glared at him. *I hope you drown,* she thought. Instantly, she felt awful for making such a terrible wish.

Michael screamed.

Kelly's heart slammed against her chest. Her brother slashed his arms down, striking at something in the water. He screamed again. Then he lurched and disappeared beneath the water.

"Michael!" Kelly ran to the edge of the ocean. She searched for any sign of her brother. She rushed into the water, unsure of what to do. "Mom! Dad! Come back! Help!" Kelly yelled toward the road. It was useless. They were gone. She ran farther out. The surf lapped at her knees. "Michael, where are you?" she called, desperately scanning the ocean.

Suddenly the water next to her exploded. A huge shape shot up from the ocean in a spray of white foam. Kelly jumped back, scraping her heel on a jagged shell. The thrashing creature next to her roared.

Then it laughed.

"That's not funny!" Kelly shouted.

"You should have seen your face." Michael laughed again as he walked back toward the sand. He left the water and plunked down on a towel.

Kelly felt trapped. She knew she wasn't supposed to be in the water, but she didn't want to join her brother. It was always that way—Michael broke the rules, and then she got in trouble.

Kelly wanted to get even. There had to be some way. Maybe she could scare him.

"Watch out for the sand sharks," she called.

"What?"

"Sand sharks," she repeated. "They'll get you."

"Don't be stupid," Michael said. "Sand sharks live in the water."

"Nope," Kelly told him. "Not around here. Around here, they live in the sand. And they hunt for boys. I read about them in the guidebook."

"Yeah, right." Michael sprawled across the beach towel.

Kelly remained in the water. She watched Michael, wondering what he would do next. She was sure he wasn't through ruining her day. He had one foot in the sand by the corner of the towel, digging in with his toes. Suddenly he jerked his leg and stuck his foot deeper.

"Help!" he screamed.

Kelly wasn't amused.

"Ow! Help!" Michael twisted around like a fish on a hook. He thrust his foot farther into the sand. "Kelly, help me!"

"Yeah, right," she said, repeating the words he'd used a moment earlier. She wasn't going to fall for his tricks twice in one day. "You'll have to do better than that."

Somehow, Michael dug his foot even deeper in the sand. Kelly was amazed that her brother would work so hard to scare her.

"Ahhhh!" He was making fake screams now, not even shouting real words. He was really flopping around. He thrashed his arms and kicked at the sand with his other foot. Then he stuck that one in, too.

Kelly wondered how long he would keep it up. He'd actually gotten his legs into the sand all the way up to the knees. She hadn't thought that would be possible. It sure looked uncomfortable. Still, it was all wasted effort. She'd never fall for such a ridiculous trick.

Twisting and wriggling, Michael managed to get buried all the way up to the top of his bathing suit. "Kelly," he said weakly.

Kelly had an idea. She decided to play along just enough to make him think she was fooled. After all, the sand shark story was her idea to begin with. "Oh, all right, I'll help you." She walked slowly toward the shore. But she promised herself she wouldn't run or scream when he leaped up and shouted. She'd just laugh at him. It would be perfect.

Kelly waded through the surf, taking small steps to make Michael wait. She enjoyed the way the water felt as it ran back to the sea, tickling her toes. Her brother was still making sounds, but they made no sense. She braced herself, knowing he would jump up and shout "Boo!" when she got close.

He didn't.

By the time Kelly reached Michael, all she could see was the top of his head. A moment later, the sand closed in over that, leaving nothing but a tiny crater.

Kelly heard a car coming down the road toward the beach. After the engine stopped, she heard car doors slamming.

"Where's Michael?" Mom called.

"He didn't feel like lunch," Kelly said as she smoothed out the shallow crater with her foot. She decided that after she ate she'd go back into the water as soon as Mom let her. She really didn't want to spend much time on the sand.

ON THE ROAD

▼

Kent spotted a license plate from Alabama. "That makes forty-nine," he said to no one in particular. He'd seen plates from every state except Hawaii.

"That's nice, dear," his mom said from the front seat.

Now what? He looked around, trying to find something to help with the numbing boredom of riding in the backseat on a long family trip. A sign on the side of the road told him they were on STATE HIGHWAY 50 WEST. The information didn't mean anything to Kent. The road numbers were hard to keep track of. That was something for parents to worry about.

"Will we be there soon?" Kent asked.

"Not much longer," his dad said.

Kent sorted through the magazines strewn across the seat next to him. He was sure he'd read them all. *How long had they been driving today?* He couldn't even remember what time they had started. It seemed like days ago.

He picked up one of the magazines and thumbed through the worn pages, looking for anything he hadn't read yet. No luck. He tried another. Finally, in the third magazine, he found a page of ads he'd skipped before. That held him for a few minutes.

"Mom, I'm bored," Kent said when he finished reading.

"Why don't you see if you can find a license plate from every state," she suggested.

"I just did that."

"How about something that starts with each letter of the alphabet? Look for something that begins with 'a,' then with 'b,' and so on. That should help you pass the time for a while."

"Okay." Kent glanced out the window to his left. There were plenty of automobiles in sight. That took care of "a." A car passed them in the fast lane. There were two kids in the backseat. A boy a couple years younger than Kent was staring out the side window, his eyes filled with emptiness. Kent looked back. The car sped past them.

"B" for "boy," he realized. And "c" for car.

On the right, a sign read: ALTERNATE ROUTE 37. It meant no more to Kent than any of the other signs. He looked around for something that started with "d."

By the time he reached the letter "m," Kent had

grown tired of the game. According to the sign up ahead, they were on an interstate highway now. He felt that he'd been traveling forever. "Dad, will we be there soon?"

"Pretty soon, now," his dad said.

"How long?" he asked. "I mean, in minutes. How many minutes?"

"Don't bother your father while he's driving," his mom said.

"But . . ." Kent let it drop. He leaned forward and looked at the dashboard. The clock needed to be set. It just kept flashing 12:00, over and over, never changing.

He tried to think back to the beginning of the day. He remembered spotting license plates. He remembered doing something before that. What was it? The game. That was it. He'd been playing a handheld video game. But the batteries had died. And before that . . . ? Kent couldn't remember.

He couldn't remember the last time they had stopped to eat. He couldn't remember the last time he had gone to the bathroom. But he wasn't hungry. And he didn't have to go.

Where are we headed? He couldn't even remember that. He realized he didn't even know if they were *going* somewhere or *coming back*. He tried to think of other trips. There'd been trips every year. There'd been short trips when they'd just driven a few miles to visit some friend of his parents. There'd been longer trips when they went on vacation. Each year, it seemed to take a bit longer. They traveled a bit farther. They spent a bit more time in the car.

How long had they been on this road? Kent looked at the passing signs, hoping for any hint of his location. There was nothing on the road ahead. "Where are we?" he asked.

"Getting there," his father said.

"Be patient," his mother said.

Kent sighed.

It started to rain, putting a fine mist on the windshield. His father switched on the wipers. Kent looked at the dashboard again. He looked at the fuel gauge. It showed slightly less than half a tank. He tried to remember the last time he had looked at it. They hadn't stopped for gas in a long time. At least, he couldn't remember the last time they'd filled the tank.

"I need batteries for my game," Kent said.

There was silence from the front seat. He wondered if his mom was angry. Finally she said, "Maybe next time we stop. You'll have to wait. Just take a nap now or something."

Kent took a nap. He woke. They were on the road. The clock flashed 12:00. The gas gauge was just below half a tank. The batteries in his game were dead. The seat next to him was covered with magazines he'd already read.

He looked out the window. There was a car with a license plate from Kentucky. Maybe he could find all the states—except Hawaii. That would help pass the time.

"There's Oklahoma," Kent announced. He saw a car from Pennsylvania next. *That's two,* he thought. This wouldn't take long at all. But at least the game would kill a little time.

Sooner or later, Kent knew, they had to get there. No trip could last forever, could it?

THE LANGUAGES OF BEASTS

▼

Mornings started out fine. Diana liked the beginning of the day, with birdsongs waking her as the whistled notes floated through her open window. She'd always lie in bed for a few minutes, just listening to the music, holding onto the pleasure until her mother's grating voice called her down for breakfast.

Why couldn't people sound like birds? Diana wondered. Or better yet, why couldn't people be silent?

Luckily her mother didn't talk much, and the birdsongs could be heard in the kitchen, so breakfast wasn't bad. The walk to school was nice. At least, the first part always gave her pleasure. Diana left the house and looked both ways, hoping to see one of the neighborhood cats. She smiled as she spotted Ragtag. He lived next door but always ran up for petting when Diana called him.

"Here, Ragtag."

The cat, lying sprawled in the morning sun, rolled to his paws and padded over. He rubbed his head against Diana's leg and purred loudly. Diana spent a minute with Ragtag, then resumed her walk to school. After another block, she paused to say hi to her next friend.

"Good morning," she said to the dog. She didn't know his name, but he was almost always there, straining at the limit of a long rope in the front yard, wagging his tail and barking.

And that was about the end of the good part of the morning. The next few blocks brought her into the crowded place, filled with people who jabbered and talked about stupid things. Diana wished there were fewer people. Wherever she looked, she saw unpleasant sights. There was a man eating a doughnut while he walked to work. Didn't he realize how revolting he looked, cramming food in his mouth, bending halfway over in an attempt to avoid getting powdered sugar on his suit? Diana shook her head and snickered at the sight. And the two women ahead of her— Diana couldn't believe how silly their conversation was. All they talked about was the television shows they'd watched the night before.

By the time she reached her school, Diana was in a crowd of chattering kids. She tried to ignore them. They were all so silly. There was Annie, who jabbered on and on about shopping. And there was Billy the Blabbermouth, who talked about nothing but baseball. Diana couldn't stand the kids in her class. They almost never said anything to her, and when they did it was something mean and cruel. But she didn't care—they were just stupid kids with nothing important to say.

The school day was miserable—it never failed to amaze her how uninteresting her teachers were— but Diana had something to look forward to. The end of the school day was not far away. Diana knew her walk home would bring her back to the animals.

When the last bell rang, Diana dashed from the school. On the way out, a redheaded girl from her neighborhood caught her eye.

"Hi," the other girl said.

Diana ignored her. She knew the girl just wanted to taunt her or make fun of her. She hurried through the crowded section of town. At the corner by the doughnut shop, she waited impatiently for the light to turn green. Around her, people talked, saying words that meant nothing.

The light changed.

As Diana was about to step from the curb, a woman cut right in front of her. Diana stumbled as she tried to avoid running into the woman.

How rude, Diana thought. Before she knew what she was doing, she reached out and grabbed the woman by the shoulder. She wanted to tell her to watch where she was going.

The woman stopped dead as Diana touched her.

A horn blasted at Diana. A car shot past them, running the light, just missing the woman.

Diana stood with her mouth open.

"You saved me," the woman said. "You saved my life." She reached toward Diana with her right hand.

Diana wanted to pull away. She wanted to escape the touch. She couldn't. She was locked in place, facing this woman, stuck to her spot as the crowds moved past like water flowing around two rocks in a stream.

"Your deepest wish," the woman said, brushing a fingertip across Diana's forehead. The finger felt dry and sharp. "What is your wish?"

At that moment, nothing else existed in the world. All Diana saw or knew was herself, the woman, and the power to have her deepest wish. Whatever she wanted—it would be hers. She knew. She believed. The words came by themselves. "The animals," she said.

The woman smiled. "Tell me—exactly."

"Their speech," Diana said, growing bolder as she heard her own words. "I want to understand them." She knew that this alone of all things would make each day of her life a joy. She would not just hear the songs and purrs and barks but would know the languages. The thought of such a talent nearly caused her to burst with anticipation. "Can you give me that?"

The woman brushed Diana's forehead again, very gently. "It is done."

The woman drifted away with the passing people.

For an instant, Diana's brain felt as if it held the heat of a thousand suns. Just as quickly, the feeling vanished. Diana was transfixed by the strangeness of the moment. The traffic light changed. It changed again. Pedestrians moved around her, talking, pushing. Diana smiled. She was sure she had the gift. She took a step. She walked, then she ran, moving away from the crowds of jabbering humans, rushing toward the animals who were her friends.

She hoped to see *him*. It would be so perfect if he was the first to speak to her. Yes. Diana trembled with wonder and expectation. There he was, a block away. He strained against the end of his leash at the edge of the lawn as she approached. "Hi, doggie," Diana said.

He barked.

"Stupid animal," he said. "Walking on two legs. How ugly and stupid. You don't even have a tail to wag."

Diana pulled her hand back. She rushed down the street, unwilling to believe the cruel words she'd heard. She stopped to catch her breath. There had to be some kind of mistake—some misunderstanding.

"You smell."

Diana looked down. Ragtag was at her feet, purring.

"You awful, stinky creature," the cat said, rubbing its head against her leg. "Even my scent can't cover your smell."

Diana ran home. Above her head, the birds called to one another.

"Look, there's that silly one with the big head."

"Watch me get her."

Something splattered on the sidewalk next to Diana as she ran.

"Look at her, can't even fly."

"Can't sing, either. Just jabber, jabber, jabber."

"Imagine going around on those thick legs."

"She sure is stupid."

Diana ran inside and slammed her door. The birdsong came through the open windows.

"Humans are so useless."

"They ruin everything."

Diana forced the window shut. She ran to her room and sat on her bed, huddling in the corner.

Quiet. It was finally quiet.

Until the whisper. "Oh no, she's back."

Another whisper. "I hate it when she's here."

"I wish we could make a giant web and be rid of them."

Diana lifted her chin from her knees and stared at the ceiling.

"What are you looking at?" the spider asked.

Across the room, an ant laughed.

Beneath the bed, a thousand tiny insects shouted at her and called her terrible names. "Worm meat!" "Stink creature!" "Sack of flesh!"

Night fell. The crickets joined in.

CLASS TRIP

▼

'd really been looking forward to our class trip. I know I'd gone there before, but I can't get enough of the Center City Science Museum. I could tell that the rest of the kids were ready, too. Everyone was full of energy when we walked into class.

That's when I saw him. "Oh no," I groaned, "not Mr. Peggler."

"Phooey," Dale said. He curled his nose and sniffed like he'd smelled something bad.

You'd think a classy private school like Wolfson Academy could afford to hire good substitutes. And, to be honest, I guess I'd have to say that most of the time they did. But Mr. Peggler was terrible. He thought he was great with kids, but he had no idea what we really liked.

This is going to ruin the trip, I thought. I'd been

looking forward to going to the museum with Ms. Howell. She was such a great teacher.

"Listen up," Mr. Peggler said. "Your teacher is out today. But don't worry, we're still going on the class trip. Isn't that wonderful?"

There was silence in the room.

"Well," Mr. Peggler said, "I'm looking forward to it. So, let's go get on that bus and have a great time."

We got on the bus. I took a nap. Morning isn't my best part of the day. When we reached the museum, Mr. Peggler led us into the lobby.

"We always go to the Hall of Mammals," I told him. "That's our favorite place." I loved seeing the bunnies and the squirrels and the other small creatures.

"Well," he said, looking around at the signs on the wall, "it's no good to get into a rut. You need to experience new things. Otherwise you'll all become creatures of habit. Ah, this is perfect," he said, pointing to one of the signs. "There's a show about to start in the planetarium."

I shook my head. "I don't think that's such a good idea."

"It's a wonderful idea," he said.

Then I saw the name of the show and a chill ran across my scalp. "I *really* don't think it's a good idea at all."

"What's wrong, afraid of the dark?" Mr. Peggler asked.

"Hardly," I said.

Before I could argue any further, he was leading everyone into the planetarium. We took our seats. The room grew dark. Mr. Peggler was sitting right next to me. "See," he said as the stars appeared projected on the ceiling. "This is wonderful. You should just relax and enjoy the show."

"Welcome to the planetarium," the taped voice of the announcer said over the loudspeaker.

"I really think we should leave," I told Mr. Peggler.

He shushed me. Okay, I thought. That's it. I'd tried. There was nothing more I could do except sit and listen to the announcer.

"Our show is called *Phases of the Moon*. If you look toward the eastern horizon, you'll see a spectacular full moon rising."

It was a fake, of course. I wasn't really sure if it would work. But it certainly did the trick. By the time the whole moon was visible over the horizon, we'd all changed. I'd tried to tell Mr. Peggler it was a bad idea taking us to the planetarium. Maybe I should have told him our secret. But what use is a secret if it gets out? And even if I'd told him we were all werewolves, he'd never have believed me. But it's true. When the full moon rises, we turn into wolves. All of us. I don't mean those pretty wolves you see in nature shows on TV—I mean snarling, raging, howling monsters.

The school should have known better than to hire him. I guess good substitutes are hard to find. Of course, by the time we get through with Mr. Peggler, he's going to be pretty hard to find, too.

COLLARED

Jay was always getting me into trouble. I mean, I got myself into trouble, but I got there by following Jay. Still, the fact that he would hang around with a younger kid like me was enough to make up for the occasional problem with parents, teachers, or other adults. It's not that we ever did anything really bad, it's just that whatever we did seemed to end up causing some kind of problem.

So, on Friday night when I met him in town, I figured nothing he suggested would surprise me.

I was wrong.

"Hey, Marty," he said when I walked up to him. He was leaning against the office building on the corner of Stoker and Main, looking tough and cool in his black leather jacket. No matter what the weather, hot or cold, Jay wore that jacket. Most of the time, he slicked back his hair, too. It looked kind of strange, sort of like in those old movies where the kids spend all their time dancing or racing their cars. But the last kid who laughed at Jay's hair ended up unable to laugh at anything for a few weeks after that. Jay didn't take disrespect from anyone. That was another nice part of hanging around with him. Nobody gave me any trouble when we were together.

"Jay," I said, giving him a handslap. "What's up?"

"We are," he said. "Up the hill."

"What? You don't mean up there, do you?" I pointed past Jay's shoulder.

He gave me a look that said "You heard right" and started walking toward Varny Street.

I almost didn't follow. *Up the hill.* There was only one meaning for that in our town. And none of us went up the hill. Not up there. Not at night.

But Jay was going.

I was torn. I'd follow Jay almost anywhere. But up the hill? I wasn't sure I could do that. The heels of his boots made a tap-tap that started talking to me. Instead of "tap-tap, tap-tap," I found myself hearing "go back, go back." The sound grew fainter; the voice became a murmur and then a memory as Jay left me behind. I waited for him to look at me. He kept walking.

While my head struggled with the decision, my legs made a choice. I jogged to catch up with him. As we climbed the long hill, I didn't speak, fearing that my voice might reveal my feelings. Varny Street starts out fine. It's lined with houses like any normal street. Then the houses give way to a few empty lots. Then the lots give way to trees. Nobody wants to build a house too close to the top.

Halfway up the hill to *there*, I finally had to say something. "Why?"

Jay turned his head toward me but didn't stop walking. "No reason," he said. Then he laughed. I thought he was done, but a moment later he said, "Maybe because no one else will."

I couldn't believe I was following him up to the old Morgan house. Even if I ignored the stories kids told, there had to be enough real dangers to make anyone with half a brain stay away. I'd bet the place was filled with rats, and the floors were rotting to pieces. I could see myself crashing through the floor, landing in the cellar. I shuddered as I saw my legs snap like toothpicks against the hard concrete. Nobody went near the Morgan house. Even the adults didn't like to walk past it. Most of them sort of whispered the name when they mentioned it at all. It was like a rule in our town—don't talk about the Morgan house.

I don't know the story. It's hard to know the story when nobody will tell it. But I knew it was a bad place. Ahead, I watched Jay. The leather of his jacket flexed as he walked, a deep black patch in the dim light from the streetlamps at the bottom of the hill.

We were almost at the top. The wind gained force, stealing the heat from my body and making me shiver. I tried to tell myself that it was only the cold that made me tremble. Jay pulled up his collar. "Leather," he said. "Nothing like it."

I hoped he wouldn't start on that. There was one area where Jay drove me crazy. He'd talk about leather and how great it was and how wonderful it felt. "It breathes," he'd say, stroking his sleeve. "Keeps you warm without getting too hot. Feels great. There's nothing like it." I just couldn't get excited about it, but I certainly wasn't going to point that out to Jay.

I looked up. We were there. The house, dark, silent, and shut tight, towered above us. Loose shingles jutted from the roof. Most of the windows were broken. All the ones I could see were covered with boards from the inside. I wished the house would collapse before we went in. I hoped it wouldn't collapse after we went in.

Jay hopped the low fence, then looked back at me and grinned. "Coming?"

I crawled over the fence, but I felt like I'd left my stomach on the sidewalk behind me. It almost felt like I'd left my spine there, too, but I managed to follow Jay up the steps to the porch.

"Locked," Jay said as he rattled the knob.

"Guess we can't get in," I said, turning back toward the street. I hadn't even reached the edge of the porch when the sound of a crash ripped through the night, hitting me like a jolt of electricity. I spun back toward Jay.

He was standing half inside the doorway. He'd rammed the old wood of the door with his shoulder. Jay bowed and swept his hand forward. "Shall we?"

"Sure." That word didn't seem to want to leave my throat. I walked into a world that reeked of dust and mildew. I had to fight to keep from coughing.

There was a click. A beam of light splashed through the dark. Jay had brought a flashlight. "Let's explore," he said, walking deeper into the place I didn't want to be.

I followed him into a large room directly beyond the front door. Not wanting to stare into the blind darkness at our sides, I tried to keep my eyes focused on the wedge of floor that was carved by Jay's light. There wasn't as much dust on the floor as I expected. At the edges of the light, I could see heavier layers of dust on the furniture.

We went deeper—through another room and along a short hall that led to a stairway. But Jay didn't go up. Instead, he walked to a door in the wall beneath the stairs. Jay opened the door and leaned inside.

"Boo!"

I jumped a mile. Jay laughed. "Down we go," he said. He headed into the cellar.

I really wanted to leave. I wanted to breathe air that wasn't heavy with dust. I wanted to stand beneath an open sky. But the rooms behind me were dark and Jay had the light.

The steps groaned beneath my feet. I knew we'd end up in a dusty rat-filled basement—a damp hole that would swallow the two of us.

"Whoa, look at this," Jay said, swinging the beam slowly across from wall to wall.

I froze on the steps.

The place was neat and clean. But that wasn't what stopped me. There was a low block of stone in the middle of the floor. A box lay on the block. I knew right away what it was.

"Let's get out of here," I said, grabbing Jay's arm. The leather of his jacket felt almost alive beneath my fingers.

Jay pulled away from me and moved to the coffin. He walked all the way around it, shining the light over every inch of the polished wooden box. "I'd heard stories," he said.

"Let's go," I said again.

"Look what I have." Jay reached into his pocket. He pulled out an object and held it up for me to see. It was a cross on a chain. Jay laughed. "Just in case. But wait, there's more." He reached inside his coat and pulled out a long wooden stake.

"Jay, you've been watching too many vampire movies."

The rest happened very fast.

There was a muffled thump. The lid of the coffin flew open.

I felt every muscle in my body try to leap up the stairs. But I couldn't move.

A dark shape burst from the coffin, snarling. It hit Jay from the side with such force he was knocked off his feet. The flashlight flew from Jay's hand and bounced along the floor, spinning crazily.

The light swept across them—Jay and the vampire.

They were on the ground, struggling. Jay was pinned facedown. The vampire had his arms around Jay and his head buried in Jay's neck. Jay was screaming.

I took a step back.

The flashlight spun slower. Near my feet, something reflected the passing beam.

The cross.

Jay was trying to hit the vampire. He'd managed to hold onto the stake, but all he could do was stab at the air.

I stepped forward, grabbed the cross, and ran to the struggling figures. I held the cross out, my hands shaking so badly I thought my bones would tear loose from their joints.

I pressed the cross against the side of the vampire's head. The skin that touched my fingers felt old and dry and dead.

There was a hiss of scorched flesh, and the room filled with a dreadful stench. The vampire sprang up, its hands clutched over its face. It stumbled against the open coffin and let out a cry unlike anything I had ever heard. Whether hunger or sorrow or anger, I couldn't tell.

Screaming his own howl, Jay struggled to his knees, the stake still gripped in his hand. He staggered to his feet, then rushed at the vampire and plunged the point into the monster's chest.

I turned my head away, but I heard the sound of the stake, like a shovel slicing into mud. When I looked again, the vampire had fallen back into the box. I ran forward and slammed down the lid, then placed the cross on top. The instant it touched the wood, it was as if a lock had snapped shut on the coffin.

I reached over to help Jay. I was afraid to take my eyes from the lid of the coffin, afraid it would fly open again. I felt leather. I grabbed and pulled and backed off, guiding Jay, leading him away. I found the flashlight with my other hand and we stumbled up the stairs.

Jay was almost all deadweight at first. By the time we reached the front room, he had recovered enough to walk without my help. We made it out of the house.

I never realized how much I loved the smell of the outdoors.

Down the street, the flashlight died. I guess something had been damaged when it fell. But we didn't need it anymore.

"Are you . . . ?" I started to ask. "Did it . . . ?"

Jay felt his neck. Then he swore.

"Did it bite you bad?" I asked. There was no doubt the creature in the basement had been a vampire. The cross, the stake, the coffin—there was no question what we had faced. And I knew that anyone bitten by a vampire would turn into one. I moved a step away from Jay, afraid he might change before my eyes.

"Relax." Jay turned and showed me the damage. His collar, in a flipped up position covering his neck, was ripped and torn. There were two holes in the leather. But I didn't see any blood.

"Just the coat?" I asked.

He nodded. "I love this coat," he said, running his fingers along the wounded section.

"Better it than you," I said.

He didn't reply.

We walked back toward town, pausing to rest on a bench at a bus stop. We were just at the edge of the wooded area. "You know what would have happened if he'd bitten you," I said.

Jay nodded.

"But we made it." I looked back up the hill at the house, still not completely believing what we'd been through, or that we had actually escaped.

"I owe you one," Jay said, touching the tears in his collar.

I didn't answer. I wasn't sure whether he was speaking to me or the coat.

We sat in silence. This was not the time to discuss the things that had happened.

I glanced at Jay. He was running his fingers inside his jacket collar. Suddenly he made a choking sound like he had swallowed something just a bit too big to get down in one piece.

The collar of his jacket rippled for an instant.

Jay must have known. He reached for the zipper. He tried. He really tried to escape. The collar snapped around his neck. The ends of the collar stabbed at his flesh. The zipper pulled tighter. Jay grabbed at his throat and gasped.

I reached out to help him. The flap of his pocket slashed at me, almost cutting my hand.

Courage goes only so deep. I ran.

But there was still some courage in me. I didn't race to the bottom of the hill. I ran for the house and the cross. I hurried through the rooms and down the steps, feeling my way through the basement in total darkness, waiting each instant for the vampire to grab me and hurl me to the floor. My hands met warm softness instead of the hard wood of the coffin. For a moment, I didn't understand. Then, thinking back to the fireplace at home, I knew what I was feeling. It had all become ashes. The vampire and his coffin—everything on the slab of stone had turned to ashes. All but the cross. My hand met the metal buried among the remains. I grabbed the cross and I ran back down the hill.

I was too late.

Jay lay on the ground, unmoving, his face pale and drained. There was a hole on each side of his neck. That tore a hole in my heart. But there was one other part much worse. There was one thing that made me clutch the cold, small cross with all my strength.

Jay's jacket was gone.

Out in the trees, in the woods beyond the bench, something rustled and fluttered.

THE SUBSTITUTE

Jane scurried through the classroom doorway and slipped into her seat just before the late bell rang. She felt her face flush as she listened to the voices of the other students and wondered how much of the chatter and laughter was aimed at her. She sank deeper into her chair and glanced toward the front of the room to see if Mr. Muller had noticed her arrival.

But Mr. Muller wasn't there.

"I'm Mr. Pringe," the man standing by the blackboard said. He paused to run a hand through his uncombed hair. "Mr. Muller couldn't be here today. I'm your substitute. I'm sure we'll all have a marvelous time."

An instant wave of excitement flowed through the class. Jane could sense the kids around her trying to figure out what they could get away with. She knew that some substitutes were like iron rods with legs, not letting the kids have any slack. Others were as easy to manipulate as wet clay. It was almost as if they wore signs saying: "Play tricks on me." That was fine with Jane. If the kids were busy torturing a substitute, they might leave her alone.

But this substitute didn't take attendance, or do anything else that gave the class an easy chance to play a trick on him. He got right to work.

"I know how much you kids like science," Mr. Pringe said, "so I've set up a little demonstration."

He reached behind the desk and hauled up a mess of wires connected to an assortment of shiny metal parts. "Now, I need a volunteer."

There was dead silence. Then, behind her, Tommy Lindstrom said, "How about Jane?"

She felt a *thunk* as he kicked the back of her chair. She wanted to turn and shout for him to stop. But she knew that if she shouted, the whole class would laugh at her—just the way kids had laughed when someone had hidden her notebook last week, or when they'd put that rubber worm in her lunch.

"Yeah, Jane," Linda Russo said, dragging out the *a* so it sounded like "Jaaaaaaaaane."

Stop it, Jane thought. *Leave me alone.* She felt her face grow red and wished she could fade into the air. She squeezed her notebook against her chest and shook her head.

Mr. Pringe was looking right at her. He extended his hand. "Come on, *Jane*, this will be fun."

Jane shook her head again. She flinched as something bounced off the back of her neck. It felt like a crumpled ball of paper.

"Well," Mr. Pringe said, tilting his head down and peering over his glasses, "I see Jane isn't interested in science." He opened a notebook, pulled a pen from his shirt pocket, and started writing. As he wrote, he spoke the words, each word isolated by a small cushion of silence. "Not . . . interested . . . in . . . science." Then he snapped the book shut and said, "Well, who would like to volunteer?"

All around Jane, hands shot up like rockets. She almost raised her own. *I could ask for another chance,* she thought. *It might not be too late.*

She dropped the idea. It would just give them another reason to laugh at her. Every time she spoke, someone found something to mock. When she walked down the halls, when she took out her lunch, when she moved or breathed or sat still, someone made fun of her.

"That's the spirit," Mr. Pringe told the class. "It's science. You'll love it."

Kids were hopping up like sprung mousetraps, waving their arms for attention. Several students rushed toward the front of the room. Everyone except Jane flowed forward.

Jane sat alone in her seat. Nobody was watching her. But she knew that eventually they'd notice her again and make their stupid comments and laugh their stupid laughs. Quietly, she stood and walked over toward the rest of the class.

"My, my, so many volunteers," Mr. Pringe said. "It would be unfair to pick just one. Let's get every *volunteer* up here." As he spoke the word *volunteer*, he stared directly at Jane.

All the kids were crowding around the substitute now. Jane looked away from Mr. Pringe's stare, wondering if it was too late to take part in the fun. It was obvious he didn't want her there.

"Everyone form a ring and join hands," the substitute said.

There was some shuffling and scuffling as kids tried to make sure they weren't stuck holding undesirable hands, but the circle was formed before Mr. Pringe had a chance to say "Quickly, now" more than once or twice.

"Here you go," he said, handing Dennis Koll a wire that was attached to the device. "Hold this." He gave a second wire to Samantha Nichols.

The kids held the wires like they were prizes. *I could do that,* Jane thought. She bit her lip and wished she could be with the others. It was especially bad to see Samantha getting to hold one of the wires. The girl was always bumping into Jane in gym class and then pretending it was an accident.

The substitute picked up a power cord and plugged his contraption into the wall socket. He held his finger over a large red button. "Now, class, we are going to do an experiment in conductivity. Oops, looks like there's a loose connection. This won't take long. I'll have it fixed in a moment. Then we can begin." He pulled a screwdriver from his pocket and started fiddling with some of the wires next to the button.

Several of the kids in the circle who faced in Jane's direction grinned at her. Tommy stuck his tongue out. Samantha actually giggled and waved the wire at Jane.

Linda wagged her head from side to side and scrunched up her nose. "Jane, Jane," she whispered, "you're a pain."

Jane watched them, all standing so happily in their circle, and something broke inside of her. She fled the room. She'd had it—enough of their taunting, enough of their mean tricks. She ran, not caring if she missed the experiment or got in trouble. She was beyond fears of anything that might happen. What more could they do to her?

She raced past the cafeteria. She ran past the gym. She started to dash past the principal's office. But she stopped when she saw the policemen. They were huddled in the entrance area. One officer was talking to the principal. Everyone seemed very serious.

"We think he might have come here," the policeman said.

"Is he dangerous?" the principal asked.

"We don't know. He's never escaped before. He imagines things. He used to be a teacher, but the students teased him so much it did something to his mind. Sometimes he likes to pretend he's still a teacher. We're checking all the schools. He might not be dangerous. He might not even be here. But we have to check."

"Please do," the principal said.

The policemen turned toward the hall. One of them linked eyes with Jane. At that instant, Jane realized the substitute wasn't a real teacher. He was someone who thought he was a teacher. He might be dangerous. That's what the policeman had just said. She saw herself opening her mouth, speaking up and saving her class. She saw herself being a hero.

"Officer," Jane said. She imagined all her classmates thanking her.

The image didn't last. As she saw them in her mind, their smiles turned ugly and mocking. All together, they stuck tongues out at her. Then they laughed. "Jane, Jane," they chanted, "got no brain."

"Yes?" the policeman asked. "What is it?"

"Oh, nothing," Jane said. She followed the policemen from a distance, watching as they stopped to check each class.

As they got close to her classroom, the lights in the hallway dimmed for an instant, as if some device had suddenly used a huge amount of electricity. The policemen paused and sniffed the air. "Kind of early to be cooking lunch," one said.

Jane just smiled.

THE VAMPIRE'S RAT

There are large rats in the basement of the apartment building where I live. That's not a problem. Rats don't bother me. There are eight hundred thirty-seven people in the building, not counting me. Eight hundred thirty-six of them are human. There's a vampire in apartment 47-D. That's not a problem, either. He doesn't bother me. No reason for him to. Kids don't have as much blood as adults.

If I was a vampire, I wouldn't bother kids, either. To tell the truth, he doesn't bother anyone in the building. I know. I've watched him. Maybe once a week, late in the night, he'll go out to dinner.

I've never followed him far from here, but I knew what he was doing. I have to be careful. He'd probably hurt me if he caught me, just to keep his secret safe. But I always followed him from at least a block away and then hung back as he disappeared deep into the city. I'd wait where I was—an hour, two hours. He'd return, moving slowly, looking satisfied, not paying attention to anyone on the street. Then he'd stay inside his apartment for a week or so.

Sometimes, he'd stop by the cellar for a rat. That's how I knew for sure he was a vampire. There are crates in the cellar. It's easy to hide behind them.

I liked to hang out there and watch the rats. If I sit real still, they don't pay any attention to me. They just run around doing rat things—sniffing, scratching, biting each other.

I'd seen him come to visit the rats lots of times. Usually, he'd drink one dry. Once in a while, he'd just take a small drink and let his victim go scurrying off. That was before.

This time, it was different.

I watched him drift down the cold concrete steps into the basement. "My pretties," he said softly.

There was skittering and sniffing, then they rushed to his call. Dozens of large, sleek rats shuffled at his feet, crawling over each other as they fought to get close to him. It reminded me of a thick, fluffy carpet. I wondered what it would be like to have the power to call animals that way.

"I choose *you*," he said, reaching down, moving as smoothly as a dancer. He raised a rat from the pack and stared into its eyes. He stroked it on the head. Then he grinned. Then he drank from it.

When he was done, he raised his head and

glanced in my direction. For a moment, I was sure he'd seen me. I wondered whether to hold still or to run. But he turned away and dropped the rat to the floor. Then he left.

I watched the other rats. I expected them to attack the fallen one. That's how rats are. And people. But they ran from it. They left it lying alone on the floor.

I went over and pushed the body with the tip of my boot. The rat was still breathing—fast and shallow. It curled around my toe, trembling. I wasn't sure if I wanted to watch it die. Another thought grabbed hold of me. Maybe if it lived it would become a vampire. *A vampire rat.* That wasn't something I could walk away from. That was something worth owning.

I grabbed the rat by the back of the neck and picked it up. I'd never touched a live rat before. It was smooth and soft, like a coat Mom once had. The rat didn't struggle. "Come along, my beauty," I said. Then I laughed at the silliness of my words.

I put the rat in a cardboard box I found in the corner of the basement. Then I went upstairs and snuck it into my room. Mom was watching TV in the living room. She never pays any attention to me when her shows are on.

I didn't sleep that night. I watched the rat. It shook and shivered. It made sad squeals and looked around with its little rat eyes.

Near morning, the shivering stopped. At first, I thought it had finally died. But then it moved its head and stared up at me. The eyes didn't look dull and empty anymore—they looked hungry.

I threw a blanket over the box and shoved it under my bed. I had a funny feeling that sunlight wouldn't be real good for the rat. That night, after the sun had set, I pulled the box back out and removed the blanket.

The rat was huddled in the middle of the box. I knew that it wasn't a normal rat any longer. In the light of my lamp, the rat didn't have a shadow. I checked to make sure Mom wasn't around, then took the box to the bathroom and tilted it toward the mirror. The rat had no reflection. For a while, I just looked back and forth from the rat in the box to the empty box in the mirror. The whole time, the rat kept watching me.

I took the box back to my room. The rat was still staring at me. "You hungry?" I asked, leaning over the box.

I got a quick answer. It wasn't an answer I liked. The rat leaped from the box, its mouth impossibly wide, showing sharp rat fangs. I put up my hand, but the rat was fast. It hit me in the chest and clutched at my shirt. I grabbed it. I struggled to yank it off. It was fighting to climb toward my neck, hissing like a snake. Suddenly, I was aware of the blood that pumped through my throat. I could feel the blood so close to the surface. I could feel how close the rat was to my throat. I could feel how close the rat was to breaking free from my grip.

I staggered back, stumbling into the table where I did my schoolwork. As I grabbed the edge to keep from falling, I felt something roll beneath my fingers.

I closed my eyes and shouted so I wouldn't see or hear what I was doing. But I felt it. I guess it had been stupid to think I could keep the rat. Stupid and dangerous.

Now, he was lying flat on the floor. The way a wooden stake kills a human vampire, my vampire rat had died with a pencil through his heart.

I took off my shirt and checked my hands and arms carefully, making sure I hadn't been bitten. I was lucky. There wasn't a scratch on me. Who knew how much it would take to turn me into a vampire? But the stress of the fight, the lack of sleep the night before—it all crashed over me at once. I dropped to the floor, not far from the rat.

I awoke several hours later as the light of the rising moon came through the window. Had it all really happened?

Yeah. The rat was still there, cold and dead. But I'd escaped. I had to get rid of the body. There were some garbage bags in the bathroom. As I left the bedroom I realized that my arms itched. By the time I got to the bathroom, I was scratching like crazy. I opened the medicine cabinet and looked for something to help itches. There wasn't anything.

I checked my arms again. They were covered with swollen red spots. Bites, it looked like. That was strange. There weren't any mosquitoes this time of year. As I started to close the door of the medicine cabinet, I realized what had bitten me.

Fleas.

Fleas from the rat. Blood-sucking fleas.

But that meant . . . My hand froze as I followed that thought to where it led. Then, slowly, I closed the door of the medicine cabinet the rest of the way and searched the mirror.

I had no reflection.

I began to feel the thirst. It was a thirst that had to be fed. I knew I was too inexperienced to venture out into the city. I felt much safer in the apartment. But that wouldn't be a problem for a while. There were eight hundred thirty-six flesh-and-blood humans in the building.

SLUGS

▼

The good part about playing ball on a dead-end street is that there isn't a lot of traffic to worry about. The bad part is that Old Lady Flugle's house is just foul of right field. When our ball went over her fence, I figured it was lost and gone. To tell the truth, I'd never really seen the woman close up or spoken to her, so it probably wasn't fair of me to think bad thoughts about her. But everyone just knew she was spooky.

"Get it, Sally," Danny said to me.

That wasn't fair, either. Just because I'd hit the ball didn't mean I should be the one to get it. "Hey," I told him, "if you'd pitch a little faster, maybe I wouldn't have such an easy time knocking it so far."

And that's where it should have ended. Nobody

expected anyone to actually go into Old Lady Flugle's yard. But Ronald, stupid, lazy, mean Ronald, had to open his big, fat mouth. "Scared, Sally?"

"I'm not scared," I said.

"Then get the ball." He stood there grinning like he'd just produced the world's greatest argument. "Go on, get it." He gave my shoulder a little push. I should have slugged him, but he was a lot bigger than me, and a lot meaner. He shouldn't even have been playing with us, but he was the only one around who didn't mind being catcher.

There was only one response that could get me off the hook. "Are *you* scared?" I asked. I looked around, then said, "Hey, Ronald's scared."

Most kids would have been ready for that, but Ronald wasn't very quick. He thought for a while, I guess, or tried to think. Finally, he said, "Am not."

Bad move, Ronald. He probably expected me to come back at him with something weak like *Are, too,* but I rushed in with the finishing touch. "Then *you* go get the ball."

"But . . ."

I knew I had him. It was perfect. There was absolutely no way for Ronald to escape my trap— until Danny spoke up and ruined it. I guess he was annoyed that I'd made fun of his pitching. "Why don't you both go get it?" he asked.

This was spinning out of control. I didn't want to go anywhere with Ronald. But it looked like I had no choice. The best I could do was to force the others to come along with us. I turned to Danny and said, "Why don't we *all* go get it?"

I figured this might make everyone decide to forget about the ball. Unfortunately, the gang seemed to be feeling adventurous today. Next thing I know, we're all creeping through the front gate of Old Lady Flugle's house, hoping to spot the ball right away and get out of there. Somehow, I was stuck in front, followed by Danny, April, Beth, and Mark, with Ronald trailing along at the rear, probably looking for a chance to slip away. I felt like one of those soldiers you see in the old movies, sneaking into the enemy camp.

"Children!"

Imagine six kids jumping straight up in the air. I know my feet left the ground. I also know my heart took longer than the rest of me to get back down to earth.

Old Lady Flugle was standing by the side of her house, holding a ladle—like the kind you dip in a punch bowl. She didn't look strange. Actually, she reminded me of the nice old lady who owns Tweety Bird in the cartoons. But one thing about her was definitely peculiar—she didn't seem surprised at all to see six kids sneaking across her lawn.

"Come, children," she said. "I have treats for you."

I glanced back at Danny. He shrugged and said, "Guess she's lonely or something."

That seemed reasonable—sort of. I started to follow her around to the backyard. Ronald shouted, "Treats, here I come," pushed me aside, and ran ahead. He caught up with Old Lady Flugle and asked, "Hey lady, what kind of treats?"

"All kinds, young man," she said. Then she patted him on the head. Yuck. His hair was always so greasy; I'd rather touch a frog.

The rest of us came more slowly. We all stopped at the edge of the backyard, huddled together, staring. There was a table in a clear area in the middle of a flower garden. There were seven chairs at the table. There were plates and cups. Seven plates. Seven cups.

Old Lady Flugle pointed toward the chairs. We took our seats. Ronald dove right in to a bowl of pretzels. The rest of us knew enough to wait and be polite, but our hostess didn't seem to mind Ronald's bad manners. "Yes, feel right at home," she said as she joined us at the table. "Be yourselves. That's what is so marvelous about children. They don't pretend to be anything other than what they are."

She filled glasses with punch and passed the drinks to us. I waited until I saw her take a sip, then tasted mine. It was that fake cherry flavor that's like really sweet candy—the kind that makes your teeth tingle. I liked it.

"Got more?" Ronald asked, holding up the empty pretzel bowl.

"Of course, dear," Old Lady Flugle said. She left for a moment.

That's when April screamed, "Yeeeeek!" and jumped up. "There's something on my chair."

It was just a garden slug, sort of like a big snail

without a shell. They're kind of slimy, but they don't hurt anyone.

"Put some salt on it," Ronald said, pointing to the shaker in the middle of the table.

I knew that salt was bad news for slugs. It sucks the moisture right out of them and they dry up. I grabbed a paper napkin from the center of the table, picked the slug off the chair, and took it to the edge of the lawn. I figured it would be safe there.

By then, our hostess had returned. "I must say, it's wonderful to have you children finally visit me. I see you pass by, but you never stop to chat." She put another bowl of pretzels in front of Ronald.

Nobody said anything. The silence, broken only by Ronald's crunching and slurping, grew uncomfortable. Finally, I spoke up. "We didn't really know you."

"I understand," she said, nodding. "And that is a fine excuse. It is perfectly reasonable to be a bit shy. Indeed, at times it is an admirable trait. But it is not reasonable or admirable to pull mischievous shenanigans. Would you believe that some hooligan once painted nasty words on my front fence?"

"I'm sure nobody meant to hurt your feelings," I said. I glanced around the table. Everyone else nodded, except Ronald, who was looking away. It was funny, but I found this woman easy to talk with. I actually started enjoying myself.

So did most of the other kids. Danny was a real clown. He made us all laugh. And April is a great listener. When Nanny Flugle—that's what she told us to call her—started telling stories about her childhood, April got real interested and asked some very good questions. I could tell that Nanny Flugle was happy we were there. She had lots of wonderful stories. But she'd had some problems, too. Someone had put holes in a couple of her windows last year with a BB gun. And some kid was always knocking over her garbage cans. It didn't seem fair that this nice old lady would be the victim of so many mean pranks.

Before I knew it, the day was almost over. "Well," Nanny Flugle said, "you children have given me a most magical experience. And now, it is my pleasure to return the favor. Some folks say that all children are animals." Her voice dropped close to a whisper. "But this is not a bad thing. It can be wonderful to be an animal."

She looked straight at me. "Child, you are brave and beautiful. You are an eagle." She wove her hands in a strange pattern. I felt dizzy for a moment.

I gripped the edge of the chair with my claws.

I spread my wings.

I flew.

It was glorious. I felt that I could soar and fly forever. But I knew it wasn't meant to last. I returned to the garden. She made her magic again and I was a girl. But I was a girl who had known the world through the eyes of an eagle.

Then Danny became a chimpanzee. I'm sure he loved it. He did stunts and climbed and frolicked until his turn ended. It was wonderful to see.

Everyone watched, amazed and amused, and, if they were like me, just a tiny bit scared. Except for Ronald, who still had his face buried in the food.

Then April became a deer. Beth, who loved to swim, became a fish in the small pond at the edge of the garden. Mark, who is quiet and extremely smart, became a fox.

"Come visit again," Nanny Flugle said after she made Mark into a boy once more.

"Hey! What about me?" Ronald looked up from the pretzel bowl, his face full of anger, his mouth full of food. "Don't I get a turn?"

Nanny Flugle smiled. "If you insist," she said.

"Yeah. I insist." He pointed at us. "They got turns. It's not fair if I don't."

"I suppose you're right." Nanny Flugle did her magic again.

"Yeeeeek!" April said again.

"Ick," I said.

Ronald had become a giant slug. I had to admit that Nanny Flugle had a knack for picking the right animal for each of us.

Danny reached toward the salt shaker. "I'm tempted," he said.

But I knew he was joking. None of us would do something to hurt anyone. Well, maybe Ronald would, but he was in no position to do much of anything.

At that moment, Ronald slid off his chair and hit the ground with a sluggy *splat*. I waited for him to crawl around or do something interesting, but he quivered like a nervous tower of Jell-O. Then he started jerking around.

"Oh dear," Nanny Flugle said. She went over and picked up the empty bowl by Ronald's seat. "He certainly did eat a lot of pretzels. Salty pretzels."

I looked at Ronald, whose slug stomach was stuffed with salt. He was shrinking before my eyes, getting smaller and full of wrinkles. I had a funny feeling he'd eaten his last snack. That made me sad.

"Cheer up," Nanny Flugle said, putting a hand on my shoulder. "I'm sure you can find another catcher for your ball games."

I guess she could read minds, too.

SNAKELAND

"This vacation stinks," Jason said for about the hundredth time that day from his prison in the backseat of the family car.

"Now, Jay," his mom said, looking over her shoulder, "you'll never have any fun with that kind of attitude."

"Why can't we go somewhere good? There's nothing to do out here." He waited, but she didn't answer. He couldn't believe they'd actually gone to a desert for vacation. A stupid *desert*. All this sand was useless without an ocean. It was a giant waste of time.

"Hey, see that sign?" his dad asked from his seat of power behind the steering wheel. "It's only four miles to Snakeland. Now that sounds like a fun place to stop. You like snakes, don't you, Jayboy?"

Jason grunted, not wanting to admit that anything on this trip could interest him.

"Okeydokey, let's go." Jason's dad turned onto the next exit ramp. He glanced toward his wife. "Do you mind?"

"I guess not."

They drove several more miles, traveling past lots of sand and little else. Up ahead, Jason spotted two buildings jutting out of the empty landscape. The sign in front of the farther one said DESERT VIEW MOTEL. *Pretty hard not to have a desert view anywhere around here,* Jason thought. The other building must be Snakeland. There was a sign between the two buildings, near the edge of the road, but it was facing the other way.

"What a dump," Jason said as they pulled into the empty Snakeland parking lot. Secretly, he was pleased by the thought that the place would disappoint his parents. Maybe a couple of bad tourist experiences would teach his dad a lesson about picking vacation spots.

"I think it's closed," his mom said, looking around.

His dad pointed to a handwritten sign that said OPEN. They walked to the door. It was unlocked. Jason noticed large words freshly painted on the outside wall of the building: COMING SOON—THE TERROR OF THE AMAZON.

Probably an anaconda, Jason thought. That would be neat to see. He'd read about those giant snakes in school. They grew to be over twenty feet long. He'd heard they could swallow other animals up whole. But there wouldn't be anything that good here. Not on this stupid vacation, and certainly not in this ridiculous roadside ripoff. Jason followed his parents into the building, where warm, damp air fell over him like a wool blanket.

"Welcome to Snakeland." A man rose from a chair against the far wall and came forward, looking at them as if he was starving and they were lunch. "Please come in. A fabulous assortment of our slithery friends await your visit. And your timing is perfect. We have a special bargain today—one child free with any two adult admissions."

"I'm not a child," Jason muttered, stepping away from the man.

"What a deal," his dad said as he pulled out his wallet.

"Wonderful, wonderful," the man said, reaching eagerly for the money. "My stupendous serpents are anxious to meet you. They are lovely, yes they are. But it pains me to tell you that my fabulous new display is not quite ready. Soon, any day, but not yet. No, not yet. Still, there is much here for you to see. "Go," he said, sweeping his right hand toward the far wall, "and see all the wonders of my reptile companions. Be sure to spend time with Percy the Python."

Jason walked through a door at the other end of the room and headed toward the exhibits. Behind him, he could still hear the man talking. "Not just snakes," he called after Jason. "Lizards, too, and even spiders. Far-flung samples of critters large and small. New exhibits all the time."

"Thrilling," Jason said, shaking his head. He

suspected he'd have had a better time staying home all summer. This place certainly couldn't be any fun. As he'd expected, Snakeland wasn't much more than a bunch of glass tanks holding snakes and other creatures. It was like a trip to a small zoo. Percy the Python was half interesting. He was pretty big, but he didn't do anything. He just lay at the bottom of his pit like a bloated garden hose.

But something else caught Jason's interest. Next to a door at the end of a hall, he saw another sign. Like the ad on the front of the building, this sign announced the Terror of the Amazon. At the bottom was a warning: NOT RECOMMENDED FOR SMALL CHILDREN. Jason decided it wouldn't hurt to sneak a quick peek, even if the exhibit wasn't ready yet. He started to open the door.

"Feeding time!"

Jason yanked his hand away from the knob and spun around. There was Mr. Reptile, or whatever his name was, holding a pair of cages filled with squirming white rats. The man was grinning. "Well, how about that? You are one lucky boy. They don't eat every day, you know. Nope. They're not like us. But today is the day. And you get to watch. No extra charge."

Jason shrugged. It beat looking at another dose of this endless scenic desert splendor. One more gorgeous sunset and he was sure he would lose his lunch. He followed the man and watched the rats start the long process of becoming snake turds. Jason didn't feel at all sorry for the rodents. Some creatures were just meant to be food. That's life.

"What about him?" Jason asked, pointing to the large python in a pit behind an iron fence.

"Maybe Percy will eat tonight," the man said. "Feeding time is over for now. Run along."

Jason finished his tour, then met up with his folks. As they were looking through the small gift shop, Jason's dad asked the man, "How's that motel up the road?"

"Just fine. Absolutely fine and dandy. Best motel around here. *Only* motel around here."

"Good. It's about time to stop for the day." Jason's dad led his family to the parking lot.

Jason looked at the cheap piece of junk he'd bought in the gift shop—a rattlesnake skull complete with fangs. "Probably died of boredom," Jason muttered as he stuck the skull in the front pocket of his shorts.

Behind them, the man was calling, "Come back soon and see the Terror of the Amazon. We're always adding new attractions. Tell your friends."

He kept talking, but his voice faded as they got in the car and drove off.

After a day in the desert heat and an hour in the dankness of Snakeland, Jason was dying for a swim.

"Where's the pool?" he asked the man at the desk.

"No pool," the man said.

"That figures," Jason muttered. As he soon found out, the motel didn't even have cable. It did have enough empty rooms so Jason got his own next door to his parents.

"This really rots," he shouted, dumping his suitcase on the bed. He looked out the window. There it was, that sign, advertising the Terror of the Amazon. Jason had come so close to getting into the display, he had to satisfy his curiosity. He knew his folks would go to sleep early. He just needed to wait . . . .

That night, when he was sure his parents were asleep, Jason slipped from his room. Even after a week in the desert, Jason still wasn't used to how cool it grew at night. He shivered as he crossed the sand toward Snakeland. For a moment, he considered going back and changing from shorts to jeans. But it didn't seem worth bothering for such a brief trip. Despite what his mom might say, a couple of minutes in shorts wouldn't kill him.

The door was still unlocked. "Hello?" Jason said, stepping inside. If the man caught him, Jason planned to explain that he was coming back to see him feed the python.

Straight ahead, Jason thought, *left, down the hall, then right.* He remembered the path to the closed room. It was just past the python. He made his way, using the moonlight that came through the windows. There was the door, straight ahead. Nothing else lay between him and the Terror of the Amazon.

"Feeding time!"

Arms wrapped around Jason, pinning his elbows to his chest. He struggled and kicked. "Let me go!"

"Time to feed the python. Percy gets tired of rabbit. You're a lucky boy. You get to watch for free," the man said, his mouth just inches from Jason's right ear. He dragged Jason toward the pit. "Even better, you get to watch from the inside." He started laughing.

Jason twisted and jerked, trying to break loose. His hand hit against his pocket, striking a hard and sharp object. The skull! He yanked it free and jabbed the fangs into the man's hand.

The man yelped and jerked his arm back. Jason, suddenly free, stumbled forward. He knew he couldn't get past the man. He raced away from him, toward the door that held the Terror of the Amazon.

He could hear the man chasing him.

Jason pushed at the door. It moved an inch, then stuck.

"No!" the man yelled.

Jason slammed his shoulder against the door. It flew open. His momentum carried him through. His first step landed on the floor. His second step met nothing but air. Jason screamed as he fell. For a sickening second he was weightless, too surprised to brace himself for whatever waited below.

A heartbeat later, Jason hit water. He went under, then splashed to the surface, coughing and choking. As he thrashed his arms, he heard the man shouting. Jason looked desperately for another door. Nothing on either side. He looked across the pool. A sheet covered the wall in front of him. Maybe there was an exit behind it.

"Get out of there!" the man yelled. "Right now!"

"No way," Jason said. With a few strong strokes, he swam to the other side. He reached to pull himself out. The floor was too high above his head. Jason barely got his hands over the edge. As he tried to struggle out, he banged his bare knee against the side of the pool. The pain was so intense, he lost his grip and fell back.

His knee stung as the water hit the wound. He reached desperately toward the edge and grabbed a handful of soft fabric. He pulled. The sheet ripped from the wall, revealing another crude, hand-painted sign.

For an instant, Jason stared at the sign. For an instant, he froze. Maybe, if he had moved sooner, things would have been different.

Large, red letters exclaimed: THE TERROR OF THE AMAZON. SEE THEM HERE. LIVE PIRANHAS. KILLER FISH THAT CAN STRIP A COW IN SECONDS. FEEDINGS AT NOON AND EIGHT. At the bottom, there was a painting of an animal, perhaps a cow, its eyes impossibly wide with fear, thrashing in a river while the water churned and boiled in fury.

Jason felt a hundred sharp stings at once.

Across the room, the man closed the door.

BURGER AND FRIES

▼

My dad owns Jumbo Burger. This is kind of cool since just about everyone eats there. It's also a pain at times because he makes me work on the weekends. Despite this minor violation of the child labor laws, our family was the picture of small town happiness, just me and Mom and Dad, living the good life selling fatty hunks of fried meat to the pleasant people of Spring Junction. Then, in less than one short month, everything changed.

The first sign of trouble appeared when I was walking home from school with my friend Tony. "Hey, Jake, what's going on over there?" Tony asked. We were passing the corner by Winchel's Mini-Mart. The store had been empty for years, ever since the big supermarket opened up across the highway. Now, the whole lot was level.

Someone had come in with a bulldozer and scraped the building off the face of the earth the way you might scrape a scab from your arm.

"Beats me." I shrugged. "Maybe they're putting in a new store."

"I hope it's a comic-book store," Tony said.

"Or a hobby shop. You know—one with a slot-car track." I thought about how great that would be. But it was more likely whatever they put up would be a convenience store.

We walked past the spot, discussing all sorts of wonderful shops we'd like to see built there.

"Want to grab a bite?" I asked when we reached Jumbo Burger.

"Sure. You don't think I hang around with you for the company, do you?"

"I always knew your friendship could be bought with burgers." I also knew he was kidding.

We went into the back and I grabbed a couple burgers from the grill. "Hey," Davey, the cook, said. "Make your own next time or I'll murder you."

"Okay. Thanks." I liked Davey. He'd been flipping burgers for my dad for years. He must have been about eighty. He'd cook all day, just stopping whenever he could to sneak out back and smoke his awful little cigars. They smelled like burning skunk tails. I don't see how anybody could do that for pleasure. His lungs must have looked like the inside of a fireplace. But he was a neat guy. He wasn't just a cook, either. He could repair most of the appliances in the kitchen and do plumbing and wiring and all sorts of stuff. I once saw him fix a customer's car using nothing but a piece of tape and a plastic fork.

I snatched a couple of sodas, with lots of ice to help us cool down from the heat. It was way warmer than usual for this time in May, and I was dripping with sweat after spending just a moment next to the grill. I took the food to one of the booths. Tony and I stuffed our faces, then headed out to see what was happening in town. When we went past the corner lot, there was a sign stuck in the ground: MONSTER BURGERS— COMING SOON.

"Monster burgers?" I said, wanting to kick down the sign. I settled for throwing a clod of dirt at it. "They can't do that. There isn't enough business in town for another burger place. And we were here first."

"Don't worry," Tony said, "no one will go there."

Boy, was he wrong.

The rest of the building went up almost as fast as the sign. By the end of the week, Monster Burgers was open for business. And they were selling their biggest burger, the Monster Triple-Decker Meat Slab, for half the price of our own Jumboriffic Jawbuster. Within two weeks, Jumbo Burger looked like a ghost town.

"I can't figure it out," my dad said, leaning on the counter and staring out at a room full of empty booths. "There's no way they can possibly sell burgers for that price. If I did that, I'd be out of business in a week. I have to find out what they're doing." He grabbed a ten from his wallet and handed it to me. "Go buy some of their burgers and bring them back."

"Sure, Dad." I went down to the corner and joined the crowd waiting to be served at Monster Burgers. There were four registers on the counter, with a person behind each. Five more people shuffled around in the back filling the orders. There was one guy out front, mopping the floor. Whatever he was using, it made the place smell like a hospital. When it was my turn, the guy behind the counter looked at me like I wasn't even there—or maybe like he wasn't even there.

He just stared at me and waited for my order. It wasn't exactly the warmest service I'd ever experienced.

"Uh, give me a Triple Slab, a Hunkburger, and a couple of Mini-meats," I said, ordering a variety of items. I scanned the menu board to see if there was anything else I should get. "What's in a Screaming Chicken Sandwich?" I asked.

"Chicken," the guy said without any change of expression on his pale face.

"How about in the Giant Shrimp Basket?"

"Shrimp."

"Does that come with fries?"

"Fries," he said.

"And I suppose the Blood-Rare Roast Beef Club has roast beef?" I asked.

The guy nodded and said, "Beef."

I could see I wasn't going to get much information from him. "That's all," I said, deciding to just get the burgers.

The guy punched some buttons on the cash register, took my money, then punched some more buttons that sent my change came sliding down a chute connected to the register. The way things were set up, it looked like the place could have been run by trained poodles.

I got my order and took it to Dad. To tell the truth, and I am ashamed to say this, the food smelled so good I was tempted to eat it on the way back.

"Let's see," Dad said, taking apart one of the burgers like a surgeon going for a gallbladder. "Standard bun . . . sauce . . . three slices of pickle . . . onion . . . lettuce." He examined each part of the burger, saving the meat for last. Then he broke open the patty. He sniffed it. He rubbed it between his fingers. He tasted a little piece. Then he shook his head. "It's good meat. I was hoping it would turn out to be something cheap. If he was using bad cuts of meat, I could understand the low prices."

I snuck a taste. It seemed fine. "How else could he keep his costs down?" I asked.

"Well, he might have gotten a good deal on the lot where he built the place. But that still wouldn't explain his prices. Maybe he has relatives working for him and he doesn't pay them."

"Could be," I said. "All the people working there looked a bit alike."

Dad shook his head again. "Let's hope he raises his prices soon. I can't take much more of this."

"He will," I said.

But he didn't. Monster Burgers kept on selling

food at prices we couldn't beat. Dad started looking real worried. Even Davey looked worried. One afternoon, I caught him out back with a pile of butts at his feet. "What's up?" I asked.

He seemed nervous. "Look," he said, "a guy's got to take care of himself. I didn't mean nothing by it."

I had no idea what he was talking about. Before I could say so, he went on.

"I was just checking. They ain't hiring cooks."

"Who isn't hiring?" I asked.

"You know—them." He motioned in the general direction of Monster Burgers.

"You asked them for a job?" It suddenly sunk in that he was talking about leaving us.

Davey stared at the ground and didn't say anything. He reminded me of a little kid who's been caught writing a swear word on the sidewalk. "You're right," I told him, "you have to look out for yourself." I wanted to make him feel better. But I did feel sort of betrayed. How could he ask the enemy for a job?

That was it! "Great idea, Davey!" I said.

"What?"

"I could get a job there and find out how they're selling burgers for so little." Even if they weren't hiring cooks, they probably needed some kind of help.

So I went to Monster Burgers and stood in line again. It was crowded, as usual. The workers behind the counter were taking orders without saying anything. The same guy was mopping the floor. When my turn came, I stepped up to the counter and asked, "Who do I see about a job?"

The guy at the register kind of jerked his head to the side. I looked over. There was a man behind the counter in the corner. He appeared to be a lot more alert than any of the workers.

"Excuse me," I called to him.

He looked over. "Yes."

I felt a sudden chill run through me. Overhead, the air-conditioning kicked in, blowing a cold gust down my back.

"Who do I see about a job here?" I expected a one-word answer, but the guy surprised me.

"I'm sorry," he told me. "We aren't hiring at the moment." His accent reminded me of an ad for one of those warm, sunny islands where people go for vacation.

I wasn't planning to take "no" for an answer. "I work real cheap," I told him. "And I'm a hard worker. Can't I at least get on a waiting list of some kind?"

He shook his head.

In the end, I did have to take "no" for an answer. He just wasn't hiring.

It didn't seem to make any sense. "Who'd want to work here anyhow?" I muttered as I walked out. "The place is freezing, and it smells funny."

"No luck?" Davey asked me when I came back to Jumbo Burgers. He was leaning over the grill, cooking a burger for one of our rare customers.

"Nope." I looked out at the empty booths.

He shrugged. "Stop worrying. Life's too short to waste it going crazy over stuff you can't change."

He stepped back from the grill and wiped his face with a cloth.

That's when it all clicked together for me. "No sweat!" I said.

Davey gave me a puzzled look. "What are you talking about?"

I shook my head. "I'm not sure. It can't be. But it has to be." I didn't want to say anything more until I had proof.

So I snuck back there at closing time and looked through the side window by the bushes. I couldn't believe what I saw the owner do. Even thinking about it made me shudder.

Thinking about it also gave me an idea how to make things right and normal again. But I couldn't handle it alone.

I went to get Davey. "Look, we can save the place. You just have to do one thing for me." I told him what I needed.

He shook his head. "I can't do that."

"Come on, it's no big deal. If you don't do it, I'm going to have to try. And I'll probably get killed. You want that to happen? You want *me* to get fried?"

Davey sighed. Finally, he said, "Okay. I should know better, but I'll do it."

We went back to Monster Burgers and Davey disconnected the power that ran into the place.

"This won't make much difference, you know," he told me when he was done. "A few things might spoil, but you'll never put him out of business this way. He probably has insurance.

"Look, just get back here before opening time

and reconnect the power. Trust me—it'll work." I couldn't tell him the real reason. There was no way he'd believe me.

"Whatever . . ." Davey shrugged and walked off.

Morning seemed to take forever to come. When the sun trickled through my window, I rushed to Monster Burgers. I could see the lights inside, so I knew that Davey had reconnected the power, leaving no evidence of our tampering. Now, I'd find out if I was right.

I crouched near some bushes and peeked inside. The owner was just finishing up making changes to the menu board. Then he walked to the freezer. I held my breath, hoping I was right.

"Well?" Someone squatted next to me.

I thought I was going to jump through the window. I clamped down my jaw to keep from shouting and spun toward the voice. It was Davey. "Well?" he asked again.

"You'll see in a second. Watch the freezer."

"But I told you—he won't go out of business if some meat spoils."

"I know. I'm not going after the meat." I stopped to watch the owner. He was opening the freezer.

From his face, I knew I was right. He staggered backward and clamped his hand over his mouth.

"Cheap labor," I said to Davey. "Very cheap labor. That had to be the answer. Last night, when I saw him marching all the workers into the freezer, I knew."

"The freezer?"

"Yup. They're zombies."

I glanced back inside to see what the owner was doing. He took several slow steps backward, his hand still clamped over his mouth. Then he turned and ran toward the door.

Davey shook his head. "No."

"Yes. Raised from the dead and slaving under his power. What a way to run a business. He didn't have to pay them. He just stuck them in the freezer every night so they wouldn't spoil. At least, that was the plan until we came along."

In the front of the building, the owner was dashing out the door. I had a feeling he would keep running, considering the mess he was leaving.

The door shut behind him, but not before some of the air inside drifted our way, telling me beyond any doubt that I was right. Until now, I'd thought Davey's cigars were the worst thing I'd ever smelled. I felt sorry for whoever had to clean up that mess. Instead of a burger and fries, I'd imagine that the only thing you could get there now would be a burger and flies.

"Come on, Davey," I said. "We'd better get back to the shop. I have a feeling business is about to pick up."

"I know what you mean," Davey said. "I'm dying to get to work."

That shook me for a second. But when I glanced back at him, he was smiling. I smiled, too. I was looking forward to the crowds. But I suspected it might be a while before I could eat another burger.

GAME OVER

inda tiptoed into her brother's room. Behind her, she could hear Cheryl giggling. "Shhh," Linda said, glancing back at her friend.

"No one's home. Why are you being so quiet?" Cheryl asked.

"Listen, I feel like he's going to jump out from behind the door and catch us." She hated sneaking into Peter's room, but she really wanted to try his new game. She knew he wouldn't share it with her, and he certainly wouldn't let her share it with her friends.

Trying not to disturb any of the piles of clothing and magazines and papers on the floor, Linda crossed the room to Peter's desk and unplugged the game player. It was the newest sixty-four-bit model, complete with a built-in flat-panel screen that popped up from the base unit. She figured her brother had probably delivered about ninety thousand newspapers to earn enough money for the game.

Out in the hall, she could hear Genna and Mimi talking. Hurrying, Linda gathered the game console, the power supply, and four joysticks. The SpaceMaster CD was already in the player. Wires dangled from her arms like an electronic octopus. "Here, take something," Linda said to Cheryl.

Cheryl grabbed the joysticks and the two girls hurried from the room.

"It that it?" Genna asked when they got into the hall.

"Yup," Linda said.

"Your room?" Mimi asked.

"No, I don't want to take any chance that Peter will catch us. He'd flip if he knew I was borrowing it." Linda thought for a moment. "Let's take it to the attic. Nobody ever goes up there." She headed down the hall.

"I hope this is good," Mimi said as they climbed the narrow steps at the end of the hallway on the second floor.

"It's supposed to be great," Cheryl said. "I heard it was better than anything that's been out so far."

Linda opened the door and felt around for the light switch. The wall was dry and dusty beneath her fingers. The light, one small bulb, barely revealed half of the attic. "Help me find a place to plug it in," she said, stepping toward the shadows.

The girls searched along the sides of the attic near the floor. "Got it," Mimi said. "Over here."

Linda carried the game to Mimi and tried to plug it in. The outlet looked old-fashioned. Linda started to force the plug.

"Maybe the wall thing is too old," Genna said. "Some stuff doesn't fit in old ones."

"It'll fit," Linda said. There was no way she was going to give up so easily. She pushed harder. A tiny spark flashed from the outlet as the plug finally sank in. "See? No problem."

They hooked up the joysticks and sat down to play. "Here goes," Linda said, pressing the on/off switch. She watched as the title page came up, spinning toward them in stunning 3-D graphics. Stereo sound surrounded them, music mixed with the whooshing of rockets.

"Cool," Mimi said. "Let's play."

Linda, with joystick number one, selected a multi-player game. In a moment, the girls were piloting four ships through a deadly field of asteroids and enemy attackers.

"Whoa, this is tough," Genna said as her ship took a hit.

Linda moved quickly to avoid a pair of asteroids, then fired at another that was closing in on her. "Got it," she said.

"Great graphics," Cheryl said. "Everything looks so real."

"Ouch, hit again," Genna said. "One more and I'm history."

Linda checked her status bar. She was doing fine. No hits yet. "Hey, let's fly in front of Genna so we can protect her," she said. Just then, Genna's ship took another hit and exploded in a spectacular fireball.

"Too late," Linda said. "Sorry, Genna."

Genna didn't answer.

"No need to sulk," Linda said. She glanced at her friend. But Genna wasn't there. "Hey, where'd she go?"

"Must have gone for a drink," Cheryl said. "Oops," she added as she got hit.

Linda turned her attention back to the game. It was funny—she didn't remember Genna leaving. But she really couldn't pay attention to anything besides the asteroids that were hurtling toward her ship—not if she wanted to stay alive. Another huge chunk of pitted rock sped toward her from the left, but she shot it just in time.

"Darn," Cheryl said. Her ship took a final hit. It turned into a fireball, then faded to nothing.

Linda heard the thud of a joystick hitting the floor. "Hey, careful with that," she said as she glanced over.

Cheryl wasn't there.

"What's going on?" Mimi said. "Where'd Cheryl go? She was right here."

"I don't know."

"That does it," Mimi said, her voice rising in pitch. "I quit." She put her joystick down and stepped back.

Her ship, unguided, took a hit.

"I'm not playing. That's not me anymore." Mimi was shouting now. She took another step back.

Her ship got hit again. And again. It exploded.

Linda risked a glance at her friend. Just as she looked, Mimi vanished from sight, turning a glowing amber like the ship and then fading into nothingness. Her ship was gone. She was gone.

Linda reached one hand toward the power switch, then yanked it back in time to steer clear of two more asteroids. She wanted to turn the game off, but she was afraid.

"Oh no!" She took a hit from an enemy ship. She fired back and blew it up before it could cause more damage.

The game was getting harder. Linda tried to pay attention, but she could barely concentrate. The joystick shook in her hands, almost as if it wanted to squirm free. Her palms grew damp and her fingers began to ache.

"No!"

Another hit. One more and her ship would explode.

A bead of sweat rolled down her forehead and into the corner of her eye. She rubbed her eye against her arm, not daring to take a hand from the joystick. Even this motion was too much. An asteroid clipped the side of her ship. The power bar slid into nothingness. The ship glowed bright red and began to expand.

Linda's thumb slid across the joystick. She felt herself fading. She hit the pause button.

The game stopped.

The word PAUSE flashed on the screen. Behind it, the ship had just begun to break apart. It was frozen for the moment, but its fate was obvious.

She heard the front door open and close. "Linda," her mom called. "Are you home?"

It was in that instant, as she tried to answer, that Linda knew what she had done. The game was halted, locked in place. So was Linda.

"Are you here?" her mom called.

She heard footsteps moving from room to room. She heard calls. The steps never came up the attic stairs. Linda was frozen, unable to answer. Eventually, the calls stopped. In front of her, the game hung suspended, waiting for someone to press a button—waiting patiently and forever.

SMUNKIES

▼

My little brother is such a jerk. But I guess that's his role at the moment. Tommy's only six, and it's tough not to be a jerk at six. My friend Brian is a jerk, too. Brian's my age, so he has no excuse.

More than anything, Tommy is a jerk about those stupid catalogs of his. He's always saving his allowance and ordering junk that anyone with half a brain would know was worthless. Most of the stuff he gets never works or doesn't do what it's supposed to do. The few things that actually worked broke right away.

Tommy never learns. Every month or so, he'll start haunting the front window, looking for the UPS truck, waiting for his order to come. The truck passes by all the time, but it usually doesn't have anything for us. Still as soon as he sees the truck, Tommy will start to dance like a dog that has to pee.

If Brian's around, he'll almost always say, "Hey, you'd better let your brother out in the yard before he messes the carpet."

Today, Brian was over. We'd been planning to put new valve-cover gaskets on Dad's junker Plymouth. Dad had offered us ten bucks each to do the job, which was just fine as far as we were concerned. We'd get up to our elbows in grease and get paid for the pleasure. What could be better?

We were standing in the driveway when the brown truck came by. This time, it squealed to a stop right in front of the house. I looked over at the window and smiled. Tommy was about to go ballistic. He was hopping so hard I thought his head would snap away from his body. Then he disappeared from the window. An instant later, he was out the door and flying down the porch. He practically pulled the box from the driver's hands, then rushed back into the house.

"Your brother needs to calm down a bit," Brian said. He pawed through the tool kit, until he found the socket wrench.

"Hey, we were young once." I sort of understood how Tommy felt.

"Yeah, but we were never that goofy."

A few minutes later, Tommy came running out. "I need a jar for my smunkies," he said.

"Smunkies?" I usually understood him, but this time I didn't have a clue.

"Look." He held up a small package.

I read the label. SEA MONKEYS, it announced in

large letters. On the back, there was a picture of these playful, happy creatures dancing around in a tank of water.

"Tommy . . ." I wanted to tell him he'd probably just spent his money on some kind of tiny shrimp. I was pretty sure that's all they were. But he looked so happy and eager, I didn't have the heart to tell him the truth.

"I need a jar," he said.

"There are plenty in the garage, right next to the rake," I told him. "Just make sure you get a clean one. Don't take one that smells like paint thinner or gasoline. Okay?" I'd hate to see his new pets going belly up—or whatever went up on them—right at the start.

"Hey," Brian walked around the car. "Whatcha got?"

"Nothing." Tommy put his hand behind his back.

"Come on, let me see."

Tommy looked at me. I shrugged. What harm could Brian do?

"Oh, wow," Brian said when he'd taken the packet from Tommy. "How very, very cool." He laughed and started to give the package back. At the last moment, he jerked his hand away. He did this a couple more times.

I could tell Tommy was about to cry. "Come on, Brian, knock it off."

Brian didn't say anything, but he held his hand still so Tommy could grab the packet. As soon as Tommy got it back, he went running off to the garage.

A minute later, I heard him calling me. "There's something wrong," he said.

I went in to see what the problem was.

"It's just sand." He pointed to the jar he'd filled with water.

"Those are eggs. They'll hatch. You have to wait a little."

"Smunkies come from eggs?" He looked at me like I'd told him spaghetti grew on trees.

"Yup. You have to wait for them to hatch."

"How long?" he asked.

"I don't know. A couple of days, maybe a week. I'm not sure."

"I bet we can speed it up."

The voice caught me by surprise. I hadn't realized Brian had walked into the garage behind me.

"You just have to know what to add." He looked around. Suddenly, his face lit up. He grabbed a box of plant fertilizer. "This will help," he said. Before I could stop him, he sprinkled some into the jar.

"Don't worry, I know what I'm doing." He grabbed a second container and shook something else into Tommy's jar. He was about to put in yet another powder when Tommy finally pulled the whole thing back, sloshing some of the water.

"Stop it! You'll kill them." He snatched a lid from the shelf and put it on the jar. The way his lip was sticking out, I knew his eyes were real close to turning into a pair of miniature waterfalls.

"Tommy, why don't you put that down and help us with the car?"

"Really?" He looked at me, his face suddenly wiped free of all sorrow.

"Sure." I shifted my gaze over to Brian, letting him know that he was in big trouble if he said a word.

So we went and changed Dad's valve-cover gaskets and got all covered with grease and had a wonderful time.

I guess I was wrong about the shrimp taking a while. They hatched during the night. Tommy came running into my room that morning to show me.

"Look—my smunkies," he said, holding up the jar. "Big smunkies."

"Yeah, they sure are big." I watched the shrimp swimming around the jar. They were large enough that I could make out their legs and eyes.

"Maybe I need a bigger jar," Tommy said.

"No, they won't grow that much."

"They might," he said. "Got a bigger jar?"

"Let's look."

We went to the cellar, where we keep all the really good junk, and searched around. I finally found an old jar that must have been left over from when Mom had decided she could save a lot of money by buying really big bunches of everything. She'd gotten this gigantic vat of mayonnaise. It took up almost a whole shelf in the fridge. I think it went bad before we'd had a chance to use up even half of it. I was glad, too. For a while, we seemed to be living on tuna salad, chicken salad, potato salad, and anything else that needed mayonnaise.

"Perfect, isn't it?" I asked Tommy when we'd found the jar.

"Yeah."

I carried it upstairs. We filled it with water from the bathtub faucet. Then I lugged it to his room and we poured in the smunkies.

I pretty much forgot all about them after that. Every couple of days, Tommy might mention them. "Smunkies are growing," he'd say, or, "I'm feeding my smunkies lots of food."

Then he asked me for a bigger jar. That wouldn't have been so bad, except he did it when Brian was over.

"Whatcha want a jar for?" Brian asked.

I shook my head, trying to signal Tommy, but he didn't see me. "Smunkies," he said. "My smunkies are real big now."

"Smunkies?" Brian asked, grinning like a true idiot. "Let's see them. Can we see them? Please? I'd love to get a look at some honest-to-goodness giant smunkies." He winked at me.

I had a feeling this was not going to turn out well. Tommy ran up to his room. I guess he was so proud and excited, he was eager to show his treasure to anyone. Brian followed right behind, chanting "Smunkies, let's see those smunkies."

"Come on, Brian," I said. "Don't mess with anything."

He turned back toward me. "Hey, relax. I just want to see these smunkies." Then he laughed.

"Don't ruin anything, okay?" I asked.

"Hey, you can trust me," he said.

We went into Tommy's room. The jar was on

the floor next to his bed. Looking from the top, you couldn't really see anything. Tommy flopped to his knees and pointed to the side of the container. Brian and I joined him.

My jaw dropped. Inside, so crammed they almost couldn't move, were Tommy's smunkies. But these were not little specks—these were huge! Some of them were half as big as my fist!

"Cool," Brian said. "Check them out." He unscrewed the lid of the jar and reached in.

An instant later, he screamed and pulled his hand back. He was always being such a jerk; I figured he'd do something like that.

"It's got me!" he screamed. He waved his hand and danced around the room like he was in pain.

"Yeah, sure," I said, not impressed. "Come on, let's get out of here."

I started to walk from the room. Brian was still screaming. Then he started smashing his hand against the wall. "Hey, stop it, you'll break something," I said.

That's when I noticed the red blotches splattered over the paint on the wall. That's also when I started to get scared. Before I could do anything, Brian stumbled into the jar and knocked it over and the rest of the smunkies got loose.

Whatever they were, they moved fast.

In a second, they were all over Brian. I did what I could to help him. I grabbed one and tried to pull it off, but it was like grabbing a rock. The thing was hard, and sharp.

"Smunkies . . ." Tommy said, standing and watching Brian smash himself into the wall.

I grabbed Tommy and ran from the room, slamming the door behind me in my panic. I took him downstairs. Over our heads, there were a couple more crashes, then silence.

"Stay here," I said to Tommy. I really didn't want to go back, but I had to see if I could help Brian. He was a total jerk, but he was my friend. I went up the stairs, feeling like I was walking on explosives, ready to turn and flee at the slightest sound. I half expected a wave of smunkies to come rushing down the steps, leaping at me and dragging me to the floor.

I made it upstairs.

Tommy's bedroom door was still closed. There was no sound, at first. When I got closer, I heard whimpering and groaning.

"Brian?" I called. I knocked on the door. It was such a stupid thing to do that I almost laughed at myself. I opened the door.

Brian was lying on the rug. He looked pretty chewed up, like someone who'd decided to use sandpaper for a washcloth. But he was alive. "You okay?" I asked.

"I've been better," he said. He slowly rose to his knees.

"Where are they?" I asked.

He jerked his hand over toward the wall. There was a jagged hole right above the baseboard. I knelt down and peeked inside, expecting to get a smunkie in my face. The hole went through to the bathroom. There was a wet, pink trail—maybe bits of smunkie slime, maybe bits of Brian. But I could see where it led.

I went out through the hall to the bathroom to make sure. The trail led into the tub. Then the trail led to the drain. They were down there, somewhere. I could imagine them, all those smunkies, resting after a nice lunch of Brian bites, doing smunkie things, maybe talking smunkie talk and planning smunkie plans.

"Smunkies gone?"

I turned toward the door. It was Tommy. He looked so sad.

"They'll be back," I said.

That cheered him up. But it didn't do much good for me. Not when I thought about all those smunkies out there in the pipes all around the house.

"Back in the jar?" Tommy asked.

I looked at the tub and the sink and the toilet. I looked at the walls. "No," I told Tommy. "I'm afraid not. I think it's our turn in the jar."

PRETTY POLLY

▼

This is so cool," Karen said. She couldn't believe what her father had done.

"It sure is," her dad said. His silly grin showed that he didn't really believe his own actions, either.

"Where'd you find it?" she asked.

"That old pet shop in town. I couldn't get over the price. These things usually cost a couple hundred dollars. The owner let me have everything for fifty dollars. Imagine that—just fifty bucks."

Karen's mother walked into the room. She didn't say anything for a minute or two. Finally, she asked, "What about Whiskers?"

"The cat will get used to it," Karen's dad said. "And Karen and I will take care of it. You won't have to do a thing. Right, Karen?"

"Right." Karen looked at the spectacular bird

her father had brought home. She was pretty sure it was an African gray parrot. "Does it talk?"

"The man said it did," her father told her.

The parrot looked at Karen, cocking his head to the side and staring at her with one eye. Then, as if to answer her, he said, "I'm a good boy. I'm a good boy."

Karen laughed and clapped her hands. She thought it was truly cool to have a talking bird in the house. A soft and furry creature brushed against her leg. She looked down at Whiskers. "Don't worry, kitty-kit, I still love you."

"Mrrreww," Whiskers answered.

Karen picked up the cat and said, "Look, this is your new friend." For an instant, Whiskers stared at the parrot. Then he hissed, leaped from her grip, and ran out of the room. Karen shrugged and turned to her dad. "The bird needs a name."

"Why don't you do it?" her dad suggested.

Karen thought for a moment. All the obvious choices came to mind. She didn't want to call the bird "Polly" or "Crackers" or "Pirate." Then she had an idea. "What about 'Safari'?"

Her dad nodded. "I like it."

"I'm a pretty bird," Safari said.

"Yes, you are," Karen agreed.

That night, as she lay in bed, Karen heard a strange noise. She sat up and listened to a scratching coming from downstairs. She went to the living room. The sound, soft and insistent, drifted from Safari's covered cage. Karen lifted the blanket.

Safari clung to the door of the cage, biting at

the latch with his beak. He stopped. He turned his head and looked at Karen. Then he lifted his left claw until it pointed straight at her.

"Kill you," the bird said.

Karen gasped and stepped back. The edge of the blanket dropped from her fingers, falling over the cage and hiding the bird. She turned and fled to her room. Minutes later, as she sat huddled in bed, she convinced herself she had been mistaken. The bird couldn't have said those awful words.

In the morning, Karen went right to the cage. She lifted the cover. "Pretty parrot," Safari squawked. "I'm a good boy. I'm pretty."

"Yes, you are," Karen said, feeling the tension drain from her body.

That night she heard the sound again. She rose from her bed and walked—as if in a dream—to the living room, drawn there by the soft *skritch* of a hard beak probing and testing a metal latch.

As she had done the night before, Karen lifted the blanket. Moonlight from the window fell onto the cage, making it seem larger than anything else in the room. Safari opened his beak, releasing his grip on the bars. "Kill you soon," the bird said.

Something brushed Karen. She jumped, and a scream came halfway out her throat.

"Mrreoww."

"Whiskers," Karen said as she grabbed her cat and ran from the room. She shut her door and climbed back into bed, hoping that sleep would rescue her from the images that were frozen in her mind. But sleep was a long time coming.

"Dad," she said at breakfast. "About Safari . . ."

Her dad smiled. "Isn't he great? I've been counting. He's already said over thirty things. Isn't that amazing? He can even sing. And he can make some animal sounds. I can't believe how smart he is."

"Great," Karen said.

That afternoon, she went to the pet store. As she opened the door the strong scent of cedar wafted over her. Inside the shop, a man was giving food to a hamster in a large glass tank. "Yes?" he asked. "Let me guess—you want to buy a turtle?"

Karen shook her head.

"What about a hamster?" He held up the animal. "They make wonderful pets." He smiled.

"My dad bought a parrot here . . . ." She wasn't sure what else to say.

The man's fingers opened, allowing the hamster to squirm back into the tank. "No, it's a mistake. I don't sell birds." His fingers clenched into fists. Scars ran across the back of both hands—deep, ugly scars.

"But he said—"

"I don't sell birds!" the man shouted. "I hate birds! They're awful creatures. Stop bothering me. Get out."

Frightened, Karen backed up a step. But she forced herself to speak again. "Help me," Karen pleaded. "Please."

The man shook his head. His face softened for a moment. "I can't."

"Please."

"Get out!" he screamed again. "Get out! Get out!"

Karen fled.

At home, in the light of day, Safari was still speaking harmless sentences. Karen stayed away from the living room.

That night, she tried not to hear the *skritch* from below. It's just a parrot, she told herself.

Skritch.

It can't hurt me.

Skritch.

It's only a stupid bird.

Skritch.

"It can't do anything to me," Karen whispered. "It can't even get out of the—"

Click.

Karen jumped from her bed and rushed across the room to shut her door. Whiskers, who'd been asleep on her blankets, looked up, let out a "Mrewww," then dashed past her feet and out into the hallway.

"Stop," Karen called. She raced after her cat. She heard the light *pat-pat* of paws running down the stairs. She followed Whiskers into the living room. The cage was still covered. Karen lifted the blanket.

The door was unlatched. The cage was empty.

"Kill you now," Safari promised from somewhere overhead.

Karen heard a flap and flutter. She ducked. Safari shot past her face. Karen stumbled into the couch and grabbed a pillow. The parrot was swooping toward her again. She swung but missed as the bird darted to the side then shot back toward her head. A claw slashed at her eyes.

The bird flew past, then turned and attacked again. Karen threw the pillow. It hit the bird. Safari fluttered to the carpet. For an instant, the bird didn't move. Then it rose and attacked her again. Karen tried to dodge. She stumbled, took a couple of steps, then tripped over the pillow.

She fell hard, headfirst, then rolled to her back. Above, the bird was diving straight at her. She swung her arms and braced for the ripping pain of the claws and beak.

A flash of black flew across her vision, brushing her face. Whiskers hit the parrot from the side. His jaws clamped on the neck of the bird.

Karen shivered as she heard a sharp crunch. Whiskers dropped the parrot on the carpet.

"I can't let you get in trouble," Karen said. She had to put the bird back in the cage. She couldn't let her dad think that Whiskers had done this. But she couldn't bear the thought of touching the body.

Karen saw the blanket on the cage. She took it off and dropped it over the bird. She grabbed the lump beneath the coarse wool cloth. It was awful, but she thought she could do it, if she did it quickly.

Karen went to the cage and managed to get the

body of the bird back inside without touching it. She closed the latch and put the blanket in place.

"Come on," Karen said to Whiskers. She returned to her room and shut the door, then crawled under the covers. Whiskers jumped to the foot of the bed.

"It's over," Karen whispered.

Her cat licked his left front paw.

"You're my favorite," she told him. "You always were."

Whiskers cocked his head slightly, as if amused, and stared at Karen with one eye.

"Kitty?" Karen said. She scrunched back against her pillows. "Pretty kitty . . ."

Whiskers opened his mouth and hissed.

JOIN THE PARTY

▼

Dan wished Saturday didn't exist. The school week was bad enough. But the existence of Saturday meant the existence of Saturday night. That's when Dan really felt it most. Walking through town, hearing other kids having fun, enjoying parties or playing games or just hanging out and talking, Dan felt like he was on the wrong side of a glass barrier.

Usually, he stayed home and watched television or read a book. Sometimes, he went for a walk. This Saturday, as spring ended and the airwaves filled with summer reruns, Dan decided to go out. The moment he opened the door, he heard laughing and shouting. One house away, at the Emersons', kids were playing in the pool.

It should be easy, Dan thought. All he had to do was walk up to Nicky Emerson and say hi and start talking. That's all. They'd been neighbors for years, but they never did anything together. That's the way it was. Dan didn't know why. Most of the time, he didn't even really mind. At least, not too much.

But Saturday nights were tough.

Dan walked.

He passed through his own neighborhood, traveling as unnoticed as a gum wrapper blowing across the pavement. He entered another part of town, where the houses were older and the streets were narrower. *I've got to change,* he thought. *This can't go on forever.* He remembered a moment from far in his past. Hiding behind his mother's legs as she'd talked to one of her friends, he'd heard her say, "Dan's shy." She'd spoken as if this explained all he was and all he'd ever be.

Dan walked.

He passed another party in a house to his right. Loud music washed over him as it spilled across the lawn. Ahead, Dan saw a group of kids coming toward him. He recognized several of them from school.

Join them, he thought. *It should be so easy. Just say hi and turn and walk the way they walked.* They reached him. He took a breath to speak. The words didn't come.

The kids passed him, talking and horsing around.

Another memory drifted into his thoughts. Another phrase spoken often in the past. *Dan doesn't make friends easily.*

Dan walked.

He started to cross the street, moving slowly, thinking about how hard it was for him to say "hi" and wondering why it seemed so easy for everyone else.

A car horn blasted through him.

Dan jumped.

The car shot by, just missing him.

Dan walked.

He wandered until he found himself near the end of a dead-end street in the oldest part of town. The other houses were dark, but one house, the final house, showed signs of life. Dan could see kids inside listening to music, their images blurred by the thin curtains that hung in the windows.

The curtains blew open for a moment in the light breeze, giving him a better view. A couple of the kids looked familiar.

"It's now or never," Dan told himself. "I'm going to do it," he whispered. He paused at the front steps, angry with his own heart for pounding so hard and betraying his anxiety. He wiped his palms against his shirt as he thought about walking up to the door.

Then he did it. He went up the steps.

He knocked. The act was more final and more frightening than stepping off the high dive for the first time.

As Dan heard the sound of his knock, he froze, realizing he couldn't just invite himself inside. He needed to think of some excuse for barging in. He decided he could just pretend he was asking for directions. That would work. But where should he ask directions to? What were the street names around here? Dan wasn't sure. He would have turned and run had he not been nailed to the ground with panic.

The door swung open. "Hi," a kid his own age said.

Dan felt the silence wrap around him like an endless roll of gauze. It was his turn to speak, but he wasn't sure if he could manage even the smallest sound. Then the word slipped from his mouth. "Hi." It seemed small and weak. But it made the next words easier. "I was walking by and saw you guys, and I wondered . . ." It was easier, but it was still the hardest thing he had ever done.

The kid smiled, melting some of Dan's fear. "Come on in. Join the party."

Dan stepped inside, amazed, now that the moment was past, that he had actually come this far. There were about a dozen kids in the room, both boys and girls. Most were around his age.

"I'm Shawn," the boy said.

Dan introduced himself.

"Well, come join the party," Shawn said again.

"Thanks." He looked at Shawn, then asked, "Do you go to Thomas Edison?"

"I used to," Shawn said.

Dan wondered whether Shawn had switched to one of the private schools. But he didn't want to be nosy. He struggled to think of something else to say.

A girl joined them. "This is Cindy," Shawn said. "And this is Dan."

"Hi, Dan." Cindy smiled.

Dan smiled back. He exchanged a few words with Cindy. She introduced Dan to a few more kids. Each new face was easier to meet. After a while, Dan began to feel comfortable at the party. He found two boys who liked swimming as much as he did. And he learned that he and Cindy had the same favorite authors.

As Dan stood in the corner of the room, talking with several of the kids, his eyes drifted back toward Shawn. The boy, as if feeling the gaze, came over toward Dan.

"It's bothering you, isn't it," Shawn said.

"What?"

"Come on, I know you're trying to think where you've seen me. Right?"

"Right," Dan admitted. "Do I know you?"

"Think back a few years."

Dan looked at Shawn and tried to picture him as he might have been a few years ago. Then he shook his head. "Nope, I guess it's my imagination." Then a thought hit him. "Wait, do you have an older brother?"

Shawn shook his head. "No. I'm an only child. But now you're on the right track."

"What do you mean?" Dan asked.

"What if you were younger, but I wasn't?"

"That doesn't make any sense," Dan said. But as the words left his lips, he realized that it did. He stared at Shawn and the name and the face and the memory slammed into him. He stumbled back, sitting hard on the couch, remembering a kid who was two years older. "Shawn Jepson. The kid who . . ." He stopped.

It couldn't be.

Shawn nodded. "Yup, the kid who fell through the ice back when you were in fourth grade. I was in sixth. Mr. Martin's class."

Dan remembered that sad winter, with the funeral, though the memory was smudged by the passage of time. Shawn had been two years older than Dan. Now he looked the same age. "You died," Dan said.

Shawn shrugged. "Yeah, that's me. And you might remember Ricky over there." He pointed to another kid. "Climbed one of those power towers and got zapped. Cindy had a heart problem. She was a year ahead of you, and she wasn't in school very much, so you probably don't remember her. I don't think you knew any of the others."

"You're *all* dead?" Numbed as he was, Dan rose from the couch.

"Yup." Shawn grinned. "That's life."

Dan closed his eyes for a moment, remembering a car that had come so close to hitting him. "Am I dead, too?"

Shawn laughed. Then he shook his head. "No, you're alive."

"Then how. . . ?" He let the sentence dangle unfinished, not sure he wanted to hear the answer. How could he see them? Why was he here?

"We just felt sorry for you," Shawn said.

Dan opened his mouth to protest. He didn't want pity. Another conversation rose from his mind. "Dan seems pretty happy by himself," his mother had told a neighbor just last week.

Dan gazed at the rest of the kids. They smiled

at him. Cindy winked. Dan stared at his own hands, as if he might disprove his existence by seeing through his flesh. Both hands were solid. "I'm not dead?"

"No." Shawn put his hand on Dan's shoulder and led him to the door. "You're alive. But the way you're living, it's hard to tell. Look, it's pretty pathetic when dead kids like us feel sorry for someone." He opened the door.

Dan stared outside, not sure he wanted to leave.

"Go on," Shawn said. "You've got a lot of living to do. Better get started."

Dan moved onto the porch. "Thanks."

"My pleasure."

Dan started to walk down the steps. Behind him, as the door was closing, he heard Shawn say, "Go out there and knock 'em dead, kid."

There was a soft click as the door closed. The sound of party music faded. Dan walked away. He wanted to see them once more before he left, but he didn't look back. He knew his future was ahead of him.

THE BILLION LEGGER

▼

Charlie threw a book at the centipede. He didn't even think, he just reacted. Across the room, halfway up the wall opposite his bed, was one of those disgusting creatures with the fuzzy body and countless rippling legs. It was the motion that had caught Charlie's eye—that smooth, flowing motion like a living piece of liquid rope. Now, under his full gaze, the bug froze, as if waiting for him to make his move. He made that move with the nearest thing at hand—two pounds of dead weight called *Fun with Verbs and Nouns*.

The book missed by less than an inch. It slammed against the wall, then dropped to the floor, lying open with its pages slowly turning.

The centipede slipped under Charlie's desk, vanishing like a slurped strand of spaghetti. Charlie rolled off the bed, dashed across the room, and peered beneath the desk. He found dust and scattered bits of junk, but no sign of insect life. Part of him was relieved that he had missed. The thought of that thing squished and dead—or worse, squished and dying—made him feel sick.

But at least it was gone. Charlie figured he'd scared it off for good.

He saw the centipede again that evening. Just as he was about to switch off his lamp, he saw a slithering intrusion on the ceiling. The bug was right over his bed—directly above his head. Charlie jumped to his feet and searched for something that could smash the life from the centipede. He grabbed his pants from the floor, thinking he could swipe at the ceiling and knock the insect down. Then he could crush it and be done with it. He looked up.

The centipede was gone.

Charlie slept poorly that night. In his dreams, a million tiny legs brushed his face.

"Mom," he asked the next morning, "do we have any bug spray?"

"Why?" she asked.

"There's a big bug in my room."

"Leave it alone," she said. "It won't hurt you."

"Mom, it's a really big bug. It's huge."

His mom sighed. Charlie could tell she wasn't going to argue further. "Look in the garage," she said.

"Thanks." Charlie found a can. The label said it was for ants and other crawling insects. *This should do the trick,* he thought as he went back to his room. He figured anything with that many legs pretty much had to crawl. But it wouldn't be crawling much longer. Charlie followed the directions, spraying all along the baseboards. Then he stuck his arm under his desk and held the nozzle down for a long time. The room filled with an interesting smell, an almost sweet smell.

"The line of death . . ." Charlie said aloud as he finished spraying. He imagined the bug falling to the ground, dropping from whatever wall it hid upon like a toy dart when the suction cup gives out. He imagined it squirming in agony as the spray destroyed its tiny brain and turned its nervous system into mush. Charlie caught his reflection in the mirror as he left the room. He hadn't realized he was smiling.

He checked his room later, eager for any sign that he had won. There were several dead bugs on the floor, but they were all spiders. That was fine with Charlie—he didn't particularly like spiders either. It was their tough luck if they got in the way of the spray.

That evening, as Charlie trudged through his homework, the centipede ran across the wall above his desk. Charlie rushed to the garage for the spray can. By the time he returned, the bug was nowhere in sight. He sprayed the wall, leaving a large, wet blotch. As he finished, he wondered if this was the same bug. It seemed longer than before.

The next day, it looked even longer as it raced across a different part of the wall.

Charlie didn't know whether there were several

centipedes or if there was one that just kept growing. The first time he'd seen it, it couldn't have been more than three inches long. Now, it looked more like five.

It kept getting longer.

And it kept refusing to die. Day after day, Charlie sprayed, until the can was empty. The bug didn't seem to be bothered by the chemical fog.

Night after night, Charlie threw books and balls and hard toys at it. He always missed. The wall was chipped and cracked in half a dozen spots. The centipede was untouched. Charlie tried hitting it with a flyswatter, a yardstick, and a dozen other weapons. Once, Charlie even took a swipe with his bare hand, not caring what the mess might feel like. He didn't come close.

The centipede grew bolder. One night, it crawled across Charlie as he slept. Each night after that, he'd wake up startled as the centipede brushed against his hand or leg or face. And each night, he'd swat at it in terror, slapping blindly at his body, then striking against the bed as he searched for the centipede in the rumpled sheets. But he always missed.

It was at least a foot long now.

Charlie had never heard of a centipede that big. *It's just a matter of time,* he told himself. The bigger it got, the easier it would be to catch. He couldn't keep missing forever.

He started sitting up in bed at night, holding a rock he'd brought in from the yard, gripping it so hard it left a pattern of craters on the flesh of his palm. One good hit—that's all he needed. But there was never any warning. It would just be there, on the wall or on the ceiling, silent as a cobweb. He never saw it crawling out from any hiding place.

It grew bigger, but it didn't grow slower. At two feet, it easily evaded his attacks. At three feet, it was still too fast to hit.

Every night now it would run across his chest, then pause for an instant as if measuring him. Charlie would wake and slash his hands out. He'd miss.

One evening Charlie woke and saw the centipede slithering across his wall like a toy train.

"Stop!" he shouted.

It stopped.

"Look," Charlie said, slowly getting out of bed. "I'm sorry about throwing that book at you. Honest. I shouldn't have done that. Leave me alone and I'll leave you alone."

The centipede didn't move. Charlie took a step closer. "Is it a deal?" He took another step. The centipede stayed where it was. Charlie kept talking, sure now that his voice was keeping the insect frozen in place. He inched closer. "I'm sorry about the spray." Another step. "We can stay out of each other's way. There's plenty of room here for both of us. Okay?" Another step. "I promise not to hurt you."

He was within reach. *Now!* he thought as he swung his hand with all his strength, smacking the wall with his palm. The impact shook the wall and stung his hand.

The centipede had shifted. The body had moved

so fast that it was, for an instant, nothing but a flexing blur. Then it fled. He'd missed. It was gone.

That night, Charlie had the worst dream yet. The centipede lay on his chest, but he couldn't hit it. He couldn't move. The dream woke Charlie, but the terror remained.

"What?" Charlie gasped, confused, only half awake. He struggled to lift his arms. Someone had tied him down. A rope was coiled around his body and across his chest.

Not a rope . . .

A centipede.

Charlie thrashed against the mattress and tried to twist free, but the centipede tightened its grip. His vision grew blurry. The walls and ceiling of his room seemed to be rippling and moving.

But everything else in the room was sharp and clear. Charlie looked again and realized what he was seeing. The walls weren't blurry. The walls were covered with centipedes. Small ones, long ones; thousands of them waited on every side of his room.

The centipedes stayed in place for a moment, as if to make sure he noticed them. Then, all at once, they moved toward the bed.

"Stop!" Charlie cried.

This time, they didn't even pause to listen.

THE BATTLE-AX

▼

Alex and I were digging in the woods above the creek, looking for worms, when we found it. I hadn't even dug that deep—maybe a foot or so—when I felt this thud. My shovel hit something hard. It was like in those cartoons where the bad guy swings a bat at the good guy and he hits a brick wall instead. Then the shock waves travel up the bat and the bad guy starts shaking all over. My hands shook with the impact, and it felt like the shakes traveled right up my arms to my shoulders, and down my back to my legs.

"Hit a rock?" Alex asked, looking up from where he was digging.

"I don't know." I pushed aside a handful of dirt. "Hey, it's some kind of metal." I moved aside more of the dirt.

"Maybe it's a treasure," Alex said, hurrying over.

"Maybe." I started digging a wider hole toward the edges of the object. Alex got on the other side and helped me.

In a moment, we had uncovered enough to know what it was. At first, we just stared at it, then stared at each other. I couldn't believe our luck. I'd bet Alex couldn't either.

"Whatcha doing?"

I spun toward my little brother, Billy, who had wandered up from the house. Billy stood far enough back so he couldn't see into the hole.

"Nothing. Go play."

"Show me," he said. "I wanna see."

I moved a step closer to Billy, making sure I was between him and the hole. "Get out."

"I'll tell Mom."

"Get out," I said again, trying to sound dangerous. "You're not going to tell her anything."

"I will, too," he said. Then he ran off.

"Think he'll tell?" Alex asked.

"Nah. He wouldn't dare. He knows I'd get him for it." I went back to the hole and knelt, running my hand along the metal. "Hey, it's shiny." I'd expected it to be old and rusted, but the blade, beneath the dirt, looked bright and polished.

I brushed off the rest of the dirt and lifted my treasure from the earth. "Wow . . ." I'd seen stuff like this in museums, but I couldn't believe I was holding a battle-ax.

"Viking?" Alex asked.

"I don't know." I had no idea where it had been made, but I knew what it had been made for. This was a battle-ax. Whether it had belonged to a Viking raider or one of the knights of the Round Table, I couldn't guess. I also had no idea how it had ended up in the woods above the river in a place that had never been visited by knights or Vikings.

"Let me see," Alex said, reaching out.

"Hang on." I wanted to study it more before handing it over. I examined the head. It looked like it had gotten a lot of use. The edge was sharp, but there were gouges and nicks in the metal. I ran my eyes down the shaft. That's when I saw the small red jewel embedded into the wood of the handle. It was set about eight inches above the end of the shaft, right where someone might grip it to swing the ax.

"Look," I said to Alex, pointing at the jewel. Then I wrapped my hand around it . . .

. . . and the battle fury grew in my heart.

All my body was filled with hate and rage. Screaming a war cry and rushing at the enemy, I swung the ax at my hated foe. Destroy him. That was my only desire. He ducked and my blade was robbed of the chance to taste its target. The metal struck a tree and sank half a head deep into the wood.

My enemy was shouting at me in a foreign tongue. I did not know his language. It did not matter. I knew the one thing that mattered. I knew I had to strike him. But the ax was stuck in this wretched tree. I struggled to wrench it free.

My enemy pushed at me. I staggered back,

fighting hard to hold my grip. But I failed. My hands slipped. I fell away . . .

. . . and landed on my butt on the ground.

"Are you crazy!" Alex shouted.

I sat where I was and tried to understand what had happened. How could I explain? It hadn't been me. When I'd touched the jewel, when I'd wrapped my hand around it, I'd become someone else.

Alex turned his back on me. "I'm not letting you play with this anymore." He reached for the ax.

"Wait."

It was too late. As I watched, he changed. Strength flooded into him—strength and a purpose. I knew what that purpose was. I jumped to my feet, wondering if I had time to knock him away from the ax.

With an awful shriek, the head tore free of the tree. Alex lunged toward me, his eyes blazing. I ran. Alex was fast, but the ax was heavy. I was sure I could stay ahead of him.

But he had far more strength than I expected. Within seconds, he had almost caught me. I looked over my shoulder. He was staring straight ahead, his eyes marking a target on my back. There was only one chance. I swerved, running for a stretch of the woods that I knew was filled with rocks and boulders.

Behind me, Alex swung his weapon. I heard steel slice through air and felt something pull at my shirt. The breeze flowed against my back where the cloth between my shoulders had been sliced open. I hopped over a small boulder, then dodged around another. From the rear I heard a battle yell. I flinched, expecting to feel the burning slash of the ax. Then the yell turned into a cry and a thud.

Not yet daring to slow, I glanced back again. My plan had worked. Alex had tripped on a boulder. The ax had gone flying from his hands, landing with a clatter a safe distance away. I stopped and tried to catch my breath.

"What . . . ?" Alex looked around, puzzled. "I didn't mean to . . ."

I nodded. "Yeah. I know. It's that thing," I said, pointing toward the ax.

"It took over," he said, still blinking his eyes and glancing around in confusion. "I was someone else."

"Me, too. When you touch the jewel . . ." I walked over and stared down at the battle-ax where it lay on top of several small rocks and a scattering of dead leaves. "We have to get rid of it."

Alex looked like he was going to argue, but then he just nodded and said, "Yeah. Where?"

"The river?"

"Good idea."

I reached toward the ax, then paused and looked at Alex. "Stand back, just in case. Far back."

He moved away from me. I touched the wooden part cautiously with one finger. No rage came over me, so I grabbed the ax in the middle of the shaft, keeping my hand far from the jewel. For an instant, I waited, ready to let go and leap away if the feeling came over me. But nothing happened. I realized I'd been holding my breath. "I think it's okay," I said to Alex.

"Yeah, but you'll understand if I don't get too close."

"Sure. Let's take it to the gorge. That's a good spot."

"Should we walk along the river?"

"No, it's quicker if we cut through the woods."

I wanted to toss the ax into the deep part of the water. That was about half a mile upriver. We'd have to climb down a small cliff if we went that way, but it would still be faster than walking along the rocky riverbank from here.

We made it to the gorge without any trouble. I paused at the top to look down. Alex stepped past me. "I'll go ahead," he said.

I waited until he was part way down, then followed. I must have been up and down the cliff a thousand times. But I'd always done it with both hands free. I never even thought that it would be a problem climbing with the ax. That is, I never thought about it until I started to slip and fall.

I just had time to shout, "Look out!" at Alex before I went tumbling.

The next instant was filled with a spinning world and a thousand flashes of pain. I bounced against dozens of hard things and one soft thing. I guess that was Alex. The world faded out for a while after I stopped falling.

When the world faded in again, I was staring up at the sky. There was a real bad pain in my left leg. "Alex?"

"I'm right here," he said, sounding pretty weak.

"I can't get up," I told him.

"Hang on." There was a pause. He groaned. Then he said, "I can sort of crawl. It'll take a while, but I think I can get help."

I heard him moving slowly, very slowly, away from me. "What happened to the ax?" I asked.

"I guess it hit the water," he said. "I'm pretty sure it went in."

At least I'd taken care of that. "I'm sorry about falling."

"Don't worry. We'll be okay. I'll get help."

"Thanks." I closed my eyes, trying to ignore the pain that was starting to shoot through every part of my body. That's when I heard Billy calling my name.

"Over here," I shouted, relieved that I wouldn't have to wait for Alex to crawl up the cliff. "Careful climbing down."

I listened for his steps. But they weren't coming from the top of the cliff. They were coming from down the river. Billy must have been walking along the bank.

"Hurry," I called. "We need help."

"I'm almost there," Billy said.

I relaxed. Billy could run home and tell our folks. I wouldn't have to spend the rest of my life lying at the bottom of the cliff. I flexed my back muscles. Things didn't seem that bad. I could feel flashes of pain in my leg. From what I knew, that was a good sign. If my back had been broken, I wouldn't have been able to feel anything. And, unlike a back, my leg could be fixed. Maybe I'd spend a couple months in a cast, but there were worse things that could happen.

A voice from outside floated into my thoughts.

"Wow," Billy said. "I found an ax."

The words took a second to filter through my mind. Then it took another second for my mind to tell my mouth what to shout. "Don't touch it!"

An instant later, I heard Alex shout the same warning.

Billy answered us. But I couldn't understand the words. They were in a strange and angry language. His steps grew closer. His shouts grew louder. I couldn't understand a single word, but I knew exactly what he meant. And I knew exactly what he wanted.

IN THE LAND OF THE LAWN WEENIES

Ours is not a typical family.

We moved to Bridgeton because, as Mom kept saying, "It's a small town with good people and an excellent school." She was pretty much right—the people were nice, and the school wasn't bad.

We could have moved wherever we wanted. My dad had written this computer program that was really popular. He sold it to some big company for a lot of money. Every three months, they'd send him another check. The more copies of the program people bought, the more money Dad got.

I guess a bunch of people bought the program, because Dad doesn't have to go to work. He spends a lot of time playing with his computer, but he also takes off whenever he feels like it so we can throw a ball around or go for a hike or rent a movie.

Mom tells everyone she has two kids, but one of them is grown. She means Dad, of course. He doesn't mind. He enjoys kid stuff. Dad's really a lot like me. We both love games, and we're both pretty smart, and we both wear glasses and are kind of skinny. Mom doesn't really mind the way Dad acts, either. Anyhow, we're not the normal Bridgeton family. I started figuring that out right after we moved here.

Every other dad in town seems to live for his lawn. The amazing thing is that they all keep to a schedule. If it rains for a few days in a row, you could bet anything that on the first sunny day, all the dads will be out mowing the grass. If the sunny day is during the week, they'll all be mowing as soon as they get home from work. If it's a weekend, they'll all be mowing by nine in the morning.

"They're all lawn weenies around here," Nick said. He's the kid who cuts our grass. I guess Dad would do it or ask me to do it, except we don't own a lawn mower. The last place we'd lived before here was an apartment. When we moved to Bridgeton, Nick had shown up at the door and offered to mow the lawn. Dad had hired him right away.

I liked Nick. We'd hang out sometimes. He lived on the other side of the tracks—where the houses weren't as pretty and the lawns were mostly weeds and dirt. "It'll happen to your dad some day," Nick said to me one afternoon as we walked out of school.

"What'll happen?"

"He'll turn into a lawn weenie. He'll get a mower, and he'll be just like the rest of them. And mowing's only the start. After that, he'll be spraying and spreading all sorts of chemicals on the grass. And when he isn't mowing, he'll be washing his car, or doing something to the fence, or some other stuff that isn't any fun at all. They all do it, but they don't enjoy it. Watch their faces."

"You're crazy," I told him.

"Look around, buddy," he said. "Take a good look around where you live. Then tell me I'm crazy."

I did look around. That weekend, I took a long walk. Every dad in sight was washing his car. Except for my dad. He was trying to hook up a radio-controlled airplane to the computer. The next morning, all the other dads were pruning trees or trimming hedges. That afternoon, they were all patching holes in their driveways—every single one of them.

And all their faces looked the same. They had no expression. Their mouths showed no emotion—not happy, not sad, not tired. Their eyes were open but not alert. They might as well have been walking in their sleep.

"Well?" Nick asked me on Monday when I saw him at school.

"You're right," I said. "It's almost scary."

"Get used to it," he said. "Nobody escapes. When they're not doing stuff around the house, they play golf. They never take their kids. They never do anything with their kids. It's only a matter of time until your family is just like the others."

I shook my head. "Not my dad. We're different. We're not like the other families."

Nick grinned, then said, "You'll see."

That afternoon, I sat in the kitchen, watching Mom make a pie. Life was good. Dad liked to do fun things. So did Mom. She played games with us. We all went for bike rides when the weather was nice. And she liked to cook. She'd gotten really good at it, too.

Just to make sure things weren't going to change, I hunted Dad down. He was in the living room, playing a video game.

I got right to the point. "Dad, do you ever feel like cutting the grass?"

"No thanks," he said, shaking his head. "Why'd you ask?"

"Just wondering." I sat down next to him, picked up a joystick, and said, "Challenge you."

"You're on," Dad said, hitting RESET so we could start a two-player game.

Life was definitely good.

Three weeks later, Nick came up to me in the park. I'd gone there to shoot some hoops after school. "Your life is over," he said.

"What?" I missed my shot. The ball kicked off the rim and bounced to the other side of the court.

"I hate to be the one to tell you this. I was at the hardware store last night. They're delivering a riding mower to your house."

"What are you talking about?"

"A Lawnmaster 3000 self-mulching mower," Nick said. "Your dad must have ordered it. I heard Mr. Barklay at the store telling that guy Vito who works for him to deliver it to your house. This is the end, good buddy."

I shook my head. "You've got to be wrong."

"No mistake," Nick said. "And the minute your dad hops on, starts it up, drops the blade, and begins cutting a path across your yard, he's going to be hooked. He's going to be sucked into the life of a lawn weenie. Then there'll be the chemicals and the car washing and all that other stuff. Your life is *over*."

It couldn't be. I wanted to hit Nick. I wanted to punch him and tell him what a liar he was. But Nick would have taken the punch without blinking and then broken me in half. Instead, I ran from the park. I didn't even go after my ball. I had to get home and stop Dad. He'd listen if I explained. The evidence was all around. I could show him. He'd believe me.

As I ran through town, I could see dozens of dads opening up garages. All around, mowers were roaring to life, getting set to eat the grass and spit out clippings. I ran. There was a dad to my right, riding across his lawn on a mower. Another to my left. They were all over.

I ran. I stumbled. My glasses went flying. There was no time to stop and search for them. I had to get home.

I ran. My breath was almost gone. Why did we have to live at the top of a hill? I forced myself up the street, pulling my body toward the house.

Ahead, too far off, I could see our garage door sliding open. I squinted. There was something large and red inside. The mower. There was someone sitting on it.

"Stop!" I yelled.

I got closer. I could barely breathe. Maybe I could reach him in time. "Don't!" I shouted.

The mower pulled onto the driveway, then turned toward the lawn. I heard the blade drop. The mower reached the edge of the grass, jolted, slowed, then started across the lawn.

"Dad! Stop!"

I raced past the edge of the yard. The world was a blur without my glasses. Drops of sweat stung my eyes. I ran in front of the mower, waving my arms. "Stop!"

The mower stopped. "What's wrong?"

I froze. I squinted. The voice. It wasn't Dad.

"What's the matter?" Mom asked from her seat on the mower. "Do you want a turn? Is that it? I don't mean to hog it to myself, but gosh, this is fun. I'll probably need all evening to get the lawn looking right. It's a shame we haven't been taking better care of it. That'll change. Guess I won't have time to cook dinner. But we can heat up something from a can. That would be fine. Well, I'd better get back to it."

Mom started up the mower again and continued cutting the grass. I stepped aside and let her pass. Her face was blank, her eyes empty.

Ours is not a typical family.

SUNBURN

Stacy and I had spent half the summer wondering about the girl on the hill. We knew she was there—sometimes we'd catch a glimpse of her through the trees—but we'd never seen her close up.

"I think she's our age," Stacy said as we sat on my front porch and looked up the hill at the house behind the trees.

"We'll find out when school starts," I said.

"Maybe. Unless she goes to private school. That's a big house. Her folks probably have a ton of money."

I hadn't thought about the possibility that she wouldn't go to our school. I couldn't stand the idea that the mystery might remain unsolved. Suddenly, I had an urgent need to meet her. It had to be now. I couldn't wait. "Hey," I said, turning toward Stacy as the idea hit me, "I know. Let's stroll up there and say hi."

"What? Just like that?"

"Sure. Why not?" I stood and walked down the porch steps. Behind me, I heard Stacy following. We went along the block to the driveway in front of the house on the hill. I'd never seen any cars come in or out. A month ago, a moving van had gone up the driveway. A few hours later, it had come back down. And that had been the only traffic.

As we started up the slope, I called out, "Hello. Anyone home?" I didn't want her to think we were sneaking around.

There was no answer. We reached the top of the driveway and I climbed the porch steps and knocked on the door. Nobody came.

"Let's get out of here," Stacy said.

"Maybe she's around back," I said.

"We can't just go walking through her property."

I could. I was sure she was in the back. I went around the side of the house, along a path that led through high bushes. She was there in the yard behind the house.

"Hi," I said.

She was lying in a lounge chair, wearing a two-piece bathing suit, her eyes closed, soaking up the sun. She didn't move. The thing that really caught my attention was the chair. It was metal—maybe aluminum or steel. I wasn't sure. But it must have been hot. There were a couple other chairs of the same kind on either side of her. I couldn't imagine lying on something like that in the sun. I touched the edge of the closest chair, then jerked my hand back from the scorching heat.

"Hi," I said a bit louder, stepping closer. Stacy stayed a few feet behind me.

The girl's eyes opened, but just the slightest bit. She didn't seem surprised or startled to see us. "I love the sun," she said.

She closed her eyes again.

"I'm Kelly," I told her. "This is my friend Stacy. We live at the bottom of the hill."

The girl just lay there with her eyes closed. I decided to give it another try. "We wanted to come up and say hi. And, uh, see if you wanted to play sometime."

She said nothing. I stood, not sure what to do. If I left, I knew I'd feel like I'd lost some sort of strange game. But if I stayed, I also felt I'd be losing.

The voice from behind startled me.

"Hey, aren't you afraid you'll get a sunburn?" Stacy said. She stepped forward and pointed at the chair.

To my surprise, the girl opened her eyes again. They still didn't open very wide—they were barely more than slits. "I never burn," she said. Then she closed her eyes.

"Everyone burns," Stacy said.

The girl didn't answer.

"Everyone burns," Stacy said again.

Oh boy. I could hear it in her voice. Stacy was probably about to lose her temper. She didn't like being ignored. I was pretty sure something would happen, but I didn't know what.

"I said, everyone burns!" Stacy shouted. She kicked the leg of the chair, jolting it.

The girl didn't open her eyes. For an instant, her tongue flicked over her lips, but her face remained emotionless.

"Hey, I'm talking to you." Stacy kicked the chair again. Sunlight flashed off of it as it shook, cutting streaks through my eyes. But the girl didn't seem to notice or care about the disturbance.

Normally, I try to calm Stacy down when she gets like this. But I was angry, too. The girl was rude. She had no right to treat us this way. We were just trying to be friendly.

I waited to see what Stacy would do next. Motioning for me to be quiet, she took another of the metal chairs and set it so the sunlight was reflecting on the girl. Then she went over and did the same thing on the other side. Both chairs bounced the harsh sunlight against the girl.

"Well," Stacy said as she stepped away from the chairs, "I guess we'll be on our way now. Bye-bye."

She walked off.

I watched the girl for another moment. She was bathed in light. She must have felt the increase in heat. Still, she didn't open her eyes. Unbelievable. I turned and followed Stacy back down the hill.

"Was she for real?" Stacy asked when we reached my porch.

"Who knows. I sure hope she doesn't go to our school."

"Maybe she just sleeps all winter," Stacy said. Then she giggled.

I laughed, to. And we said some more nasty and

funny things about the girl on the hill. But later, as the sun was moving well past its highest and hottest position, I started to worry.

"Maybe you shouldn't have done that," I told Stacy. "She might get a bad burn." I imagined her sizzling like a strip of bacon, slowly curling up in a pan.

"Hey, you heard her. She never burns."

"Still . . ." I felt bad. "Look, she wasn't nice to us, but that doesn't mean we should let her get hurt." I knew I had to go back and make sure she was okay.

"Coming?" I asked Stacy.

"No thanks."

So I went up the hill by myself this time. As I walked, I kept getting images of a slab of burned meat lying on a metal chair. Despite the heat, I started to jog, then run. I had a feeling something terrible had happened.

I made noise and called out, like before, just to make sure nobody thought I was sneaking around.

She wasn't in front. She wasn't inside.

She was still in the back. It looked like she hadn't moved. It looked like not one single hair had shifted.

She was exactly as she had been before—except that her skin had turned red. For a moment, I couldn't even speak. From the times I'd been sunburned, I knew that this was the start of something awful.

"Hey, wake up. Come on. You got burned." I reached to shake her shoulder, but stopped. I was afraid to touch her—afraid of the agony it would bring. Her shoulder was worse than just red. There were blisters and small cracks with black edges. How could she just lie there?

She opened her eyes. Then she smiled. "I told you, I never burn."

She reached up and grabbed my wrist. Her whole arm was red and cracked. "But look at you," I said.

She shook her head. "I don't burn," she told me again.

Something was happening to her skin. First along her arm, then all over her body, her skin was crinkling and curling and flaking off.

"None of us burns," she said.

There was something underneath her skin, just beginning to show itself.

"But if I get too much sun, I do shed," she said as the flesh dropped from her body and her face. Beneath, there were soft scales, not yet hardened by exposure to the sun.

I tried to pull away. She was too strong.

"It doesn't hurt," she said. "Shedding doesn't hurt at all."

Her eyes locked with mine. I couldn't move.

"But it really builds up an appetite."

She must have squeezed my wrist harder, because I heard a crunch. But I didn't feel anything. I just looked at those eyes, and the tongue, split and slithery, that flickered out from between her lips.

Her eyes, now fully opened, gleamed in the sunlight.

THIN SILK

▼

Steven had been in the vacation cabin for a week, and he'd finally run out of things to do. It wouldn't have been so bad if this was the last day, but his parents had rented the place for a month—a whole, incredibly mind-numbing, endless month.

"I'm bored, Mom," Steven said.

"But there's so much out here," his mother told him. "Why don't you go fishing with your father?"

Steven just stared at his mother. His father wasn't any fun when he fished. He was so intent on catching a stupid fish that he never stayed in one spot for more than a minute or two. He'd stop the boat, cast out, then reel in his line right away if he didn't get a bite. Then he'd zoom the boat over to another spot that seemed exactly like the spot he'd just left. Needless to say, he never caught anything. Steven didn't think he could stand a dose of that kind of excitement.

"Well," his mother said, looking around the cabin, "maybe you could do some sort of outdoor craft."

"What?" Steven asked.

"You know. A Scout thing. Make a tepee. Trap a beaver. I don't know, Steven. You're smart. You'll think of something."

At that moment, Steven did think of something. He thought how wonderful it would be to go back home. Yeah, home sounded perfect. There was a key hidden under the mat by the front door. Steven could just see himself going home and hanging out with a bowl of ice cream and three weeks of uninterrupted television. It would be just like that movie where the kid was left home by his parents. "Maybe I'll take a walk," he said.

"Now that's a wonderful idea," his mother said. "Go enjoy the woods."

Steven stepped out of the cabin and glanced around. As far as he could remember, the dirt road in front of the cabin ran for miles, twisting and turning and then finally reaching a gravel road that eventually went to the highway. That was too long a trip. Steven was pretty sure he could get to the highway a lot faster by cutting through the forest.

He hadn't gone more than five steps into the woods when something thin and fine fell across his face, touching him so lightly that it almost wasn't there at all.

"Yuck," Steven said, wiping at the strand of spider's silk. "I hate that stuff."

A few more steps and he ran into another strand. "I hope this messes up your stupid web," he said as he rubbed his face. He smiled as he thought of himself crashing like a giant through the world of the tiny spiders, wiping out hours of their work with a single step.

Steven managed to avoid the next strand. It was part of a larger web. He ducked under it, then paused for a moment to watch a trapped beetle struggling against the sticky threads. "Tough luck," he said as he walked on—right into another unseen piece.

This place must be lousy with spiders, Steven thought, wiping at his face again. *Good thing I'm not a little bug.* He kept walking.

Every two or three steps, he felt another strand break across his face or arms. It was starting to annoy him, but he knew it would all be worth the effort once he got out of the wilderness and made his way back home.

The bushes rustled far behind him. Steven spun around and scanned the woods. There was nothing in sight. He walked on, breaking through more strands.

He heard the sound again—louder and closer. Steven picked up his pace, walking faster. At this higher speed, he ran into more strands. He didn't even bother wiping all of them away now. He just wanted to get to the road.

The sound grew closer. Steven glanced back. Something large was scurrying along the forest floor. He started to run. The thing behind him scurried faster.

"Leave me alone!" he said.

He ran.

It followed.

Steven glanced back again. He almost stumbled as he caught sight of the spider. It was huge—as big as a dog. "Get away from me!" he screamed, recoiling from the sight. He ran full out. Behind, the scurrying seemed to drop back.

He was whipping through the woods now, hitting fine strands of silk with almost every stride. With one hand, he kept wiping at his face. The sounds were growing dimmer. *I beat it,* he thought. *I'm faster.*

He shuddered at the idea of being anywhere near such an unnatural insect. But he knew now that he'd be able to escape.

Without slowing, Steven risked a look back. He'd gained some distance. The spider was nearly out of sight. He stared at it for an instant. It was an instant too long. As Steven looked ahead again, he stumbled toward a tree.

He thrust a hand out to protect himself. It stuck.

His shirt, covered with thousands of thin strands, was glued to the tree. Steven pushed with his other hand. It stuck, too.

He tried to turn to see the spider. He couldn't get his head around far enough. But that didn't matter. Steven knew exactly where the spider was. He could hear it. And it wasn't rushing anymore. It was coming slowly, taking its time. There was no hurry. Steven wasn't going anywhere.

THE WITCH'S MONKEY

▼

I've always loved monkeys. I don't mean chimps—everyone likes chimps. I mean monkeys. All of them. I love the cute ones with their little paws and adorable faces. And I love the ugly ones, the ones that look like nature made a mistake or was playing a joke. I've got all kinds of toy monkeys; stuffed, wood, plastic, even ceramic. I've got a whole shelf of monkey books. I watch *The Wizard of Oz* every single time it's on TV, just for those fabulous flying monkeys. My parents seem to be amused by all this, though I suspect it's their hope that I'll outgrow my fascination sooner or later. I won't.

The nearest zoo is pretty far from here, so I don't get to see live monkeys very often. I'm lucky if I get there twice a year. That's why my ears perked up when I overheard Sarah Morton on the playground saying, "She's got a monkey in a cage."

"Who?" I asked, feeling my pulse grow faster as I pushed into the ring of girls clustered around Sarah.

She glared at me for interrupting her. I was afraid she wasn't going to answer my question. But I guess she couldn't resist showing off her knowledge. "The Crow Lady," Sarah said.

"No way." I shook my head, feeling a tingle like someone had brushed a feather across my shoulder blades.

"It's true," Sarah said. "Tommy Lucas told me. His brother saw it. He went up on her porch on a bet. He looked in the window and saw a monkey in a cage." She stared down at me, daring me to call her a liar.

I walked away. Behind my back, I heard Sarah making monkey sounds. They all liked to make fun of me. I didn't care. They're jealous because I have something I really cherish. Maybe they'd be nicer to me if I didn't talk so much about monkeys and wear earrings shaped like monkeys and T-shirts with pictures of monkeys, but I'm not going to change just because of them. I have a passion. All they have is toys and dolls and dress-up and stupid stuff like that. All they have for pets are cats or dogs. Those aren't any good. Cats and dogs are always running off and disappearing. I wouldn't want one even if someone gave it to me.

I thought about Sarah's words. *The Crow Lady.* Could she really have a monkey? It was possible.

But there were so many stories—all kinds of stories. She lived by herself in a spooky old house. No one ever saw her in town. There were crows all over the property. Hundreds of crows hung out there—it was like a mall for birds. The house was falling apart, the yard was a mess of weeds, and the whole place was decorated with crow droppings.

Kids said lots of different things about her. So did our parents. I'd heard that she'd shot her husband. I'd also heard that she'd poisoned him. I'd heard that she'd had five children and they'd all vanished. Other kids claimed she'd always lived alone.

But if she really had a monkey, none of that mattered. I had to see it. Chores and homework kept me from going there right after school. I guess I needed time to work up the courage, too. But tomorrow was Saturday. I promised myself I would visit the Crow Lady's house in the morning.

I didn't sleep much that night. I was too excited, knowing there was a monkey not far from me.

Morning finally came. After a quick bowl of cereal—despite what everyone might say, I don't live on bananas—it was time to see the monkey. Maybe, I told myself as I headed out, the Crow Lady is just a nice, lonely old woman. Maybe she'll be thrilled to have company and will let me play with her monkey. Maybe it's becoming too much for her to care for and she'll give it to me.

Wrapped in my thoughts, I reached the Crow Lady's house at the end of Spruce Street. There was an iron fence in front, but the gate had rusted off its hinges long ago. I went up the walkway. Leaves and small twigs crunched beneath my feet. Tall grass and weeds crept from the yard onto the cracked concrete. Ahead, the porch was coated in chipped and blistering gray paint. The railing leaned out, waiting for the next strong wind to shove it over.

Crows gathered on every inch of the walkway. They hopped aside when I came close, then scuttered back to where they'd been. It was odd— there didn't seem to be any squirrels. Everywhere else there were lots of squirrels. Here, nothing but crows.

I took a deep breath and put my foot on the first step. I paused there for an instant, but I knew that if I waited to find more courage I would never reach the door. *Here goes.* I pushed myself up the steps. The old wood creaked beneath my feet. One board tilted, rocking slightly under my shoe.

I was on the porch, right in front of the door. There were small windows to the right of the door, running from the floor to the ceiling. A couple of the panes were cracked. One was missing, replaced by a piece of cardboard and old, yellowing tape.

I wasn't sure whether to peek through a window or knock on the door. If I tried to look and she caught me, she would never let me inside. But if I knocked and she told me to go away, I wouldn't get a chance to see the monkey, either.

The door opened.

A hand snaked out and clamped around my wrist. I gasped as I felt the finger bones grating against my flesh like a trap made of dried sticks. I looked up into the face of the Crow Lady. This close, I couldn't even tell her age. She might have been the same age as my mom; she might have been older than my grandmother. But her face was hard; it was full of meanness, like someone who was always looking for a reason to be angry.

"What do you want?" she asked. Her voice was barely louder than the crackle of dead leaves on the ground.

"I . . . uh . . ."

"Are you selling cookies? I don't want any cookies. I hate cookies."

"Yeah, cookies . . ." I looked past her and forgot everything else. Behind her, across the room in the far corner, was the most wonderful, gorgeous, beautiful monkey I had ever seen—a gibbon with dark fur and white paws. My heart melted. The poor creature was crammed into a cage just big enough for a large dog. It looked at me and bared its teeth. I tried to take a step toward it, but the Crow Lady tightened her grip on my wrist.

"I said I don't want any cookies."

"Sure, okay." I pulled back. She held on to me for an instant, then let go. I stumbled, almost falling off the porch. The door slammed. I turned and ran. Crows scattered and took flight all around me in an explosion of frantic wings and wild caws. I didn't slow down until I reached home.

That poor monkey. I had to do something for it. It must be miserable in that small cage. I had to set it free. I couldn't wait. I'd do it tonight.

A million endings wove through my mind as I waited for evening. I saw myself setting the wonderful monkey free. I saw myself bringing it home. I saw myself running away with it to the jungle, far from the people who didn't understand, far from the ignorant kids who laughed at my devotion. I would hug it and it would hug me back, and we would be happy.

When I returned an hour after sunset, the house was dark except for one light on the second floor. I waited. At least the crows had gone to sleep. Finally, that last light went out.

I must have spent half an hour making my way to the door. Every step I took, leaves crackled beneath my feet. Every board creaked, every twig snapped. I kept waiting for the light to flare back on.

It didn't.

Finally, I had my hand on the knob. It turned. I pushed, but the door didn't open. It was locked. I looked at the piece of cardboard that was taped where the window had been and realized it was at the same height as the doorknob.

I don't believe I'm doing this, I thought as I pressed my fingers against the cardboard. It fell free with barely a protest as the old tape pulled loose.

Inside, across the room, the monkey made a quiet sound—almost a sob.

"I'm coming," I whispered as quietly as I could.

I reached through the window frame and turned the lock. The click echoed through the house like an explosion. I waited a minute, then opened the door.

I felt as if I had stepped into a cave, but the whimpers of the monkey guided me to the cage. My eyes began to adjust. My lovely monkey gripped the bars and stared at me, still crying those sad sobs.

I stuck a finger through the bars and scratched its head. "You'll be out in a minute," I whispered. It almost seemed to purr.

I lifted the latch, flinching at the light scrape of metal against metal. The door flipped open. "Come here," I whispered.

The monkey jumped into my waiting arms. I couldn't imagine a happier moment. I hugged it. It looked up at me. It wrapped its arms around my neck and hugged me back. It kissed my cheek. I felt the thrill of knowing that all my dreams and wishes had come true. This was the most glorious moment of my life.

"You're mine," I said.

The pain ripped through my face in a blinding flash.

"Awwwww—!"

I screamed before I could stop myself. I pulled at the monkey. Its paws tangled in my hair. Its teeth dug into my cheek.

Behind me, rising above my screams, I heard sounds like roaring winds. I spun, still trying to pull the monkey from my face.

She came down the stairs and faced me. Her expression filled me with such fear that, for an instant, I forgot the pain that burned across my face. Never had I seen so much hate in someone's eyes.

The wind flung the door open with a crash and blasted through the house. Crows flooded in, filling the air. The monkey screeched and leaped from my face. It escaped through the door in an instant.

The Crow Lady howled in rage. She started shouting words I didn't understand. She stepped closer. Spit flew from her lips as she yelled. It burned where it touched my face. I raised my hand to my cheek, feeling a jagged rip in my flesh from the monkey's teeth.

I looked at my hand. The world froze for an instant as the strangeness of what I saw sank into my numbed mind. This wasn't my hand. It couldn't be. It was changing, growing smaller and darker. I couldn't watch. I closed my eyes. But I could still feel the change as it spread across my body. I screamed again and everything faded inward until the world was blackness.

The Crow Lady's voice woke me. "You'll do," she said in a soothing tone as she leaned over me. "Not as pretty as the last, not as smart as my crows, but you'll be mine nonetheless." She looked around the room, then back at me. Crows were perched everywhere. They walked across the floor and pecked at the rug. "Cats and dogs are crows," she said. "And squirrels are crows. But children are special."

She stood straight and I realized she towered above me. The world had changed. It was larger. Strange smells, sharp and strong, flooded over me. All my senses were different. I grabbed the bars with my paws. The cage seemed much bigger now that I was inside it. I felt my tail flicker behind me. I tried to speak, but my throat and tongue could no longer form human words. So I screamed. And then I sobbed.

AS YOU SAY

▼

I had no idea Tonya had all that power. None of us knew. If we did, we never would have taken her doll and teased her. We thought she was a normal kid like the rest of us. Still, considering the basically harmless nature of our behavior, I think her reaction was way too extreme. I've had a lot of time to think about it, and I'm pretty sure she went too far.

"A curse on all of you," she shouted, pointing at us while we tossed her doll around.

I sort of laughed. I know the others did. I could hear Larry's loud laugh, along with Ken's. Mike was chuckling. I'm sure Terry was laughing, too. But I felt a bit sorry for Tonya. So I reached over and grabbed the doll from Mike and threw it back to her.

"We were just having some fun," I said.

"A curse," she said again, ignoring the doll that lay crumpled at her feet. "Beware what you say, beware what you do. From this moment on, all your words will come true."

"Oh wow, what a curse," Larry said. He laughed even louder. Then he turned away from her and said, "Come on, let's get out of here."

I waved at the gnats that had gathered around my head, then followed the rest of the gang. The bugs were bad this year.

"Did you hear her?" Mike said. "She really has a wild imagination. A curse. Hah." He swiped at the bugs.

I looked back. Tonya was still there, watching us, smiling. Something about the sight made me shiver. But it was stupid to worry about things that can't exist. I certainly didn't believe in curses.

Until two minutes later.

That's when Larry waved at his head and said, "These bugs are eating me alive."

The next part is a bit hard to describe. Suddenly, there was a cloud of gnats around him. Then more. And then even more. In seconds, Larry was covered with gnats. There was this big, black, buzzing Larry-shaped mass of insects. Then the gnats flew away. They left nothing behind. Larry was gone.

The rest of us just stared at each other for a moment. Mike, who never could keep his mouth shut, was the next to speak. "She did it," he said. "It's real . . . the curse. I'm sunk."

The instant the words left his lips, I knew he

was in deep trouble. I suspect it took Mike a second longer than that to catch on, but by the time he did, he was already up to his ankles in the ground and sinking fast.

That was it for him. He sank from sight. The ground swallowed him like pudding swallows a spoon. He left no more of a trace than Larry.

We stood there, afraid to talk.

"Any ideas?" Ken finally said. He and Terry looked at me. I was supposed to be the smart one in the group. At the moment, I wasn't feeling very wise.

"We could apologize to her," I suggested, speaking carefully and making sure my words had no double meanings that the curse could feast on.

They nodded. That seemed like a good idea all around. We walked, in silence, back to where Tonya had been. She wasn't there.

"Now what?" Terry asked.

That's when I came up with the answer. "I am no longer cursed," I said. It was that simple.

Ken and Terry watched me, as if they expected something awful to happen. But I was pretty sure my idea had worked. I had to test it. I held out my hand. "I'm holding a baseball," I said.

Nothing happened. Relief washed over me. "You try it," I told Terry.

"There's a baseball in my hand," he said.

Again, I was the first one to realize the mistake. Terry held his hand up, staring in obvious disbelief. He should have said he was holding a baseball. Instead, he'd said there was one *in* his hand. And there was. He had this huge, swollen lump bulging from his palm. I could almost see the stitches on the ball through the tightly stretched skin. It must have hurt. The way he went screaming down the street, I'm sure it hurt.

"Hey," Ken said after Terry had raced far enough away that we couldn't hear him anymore. "At least we know you cured yourself. I just have to do the same thing. I hate to lose this power, but I guess it's pretty dangerous."

"Yeah," I agreed. "This isn't the kind of thing we want to fool around with. One slip and something terrible could happen." I was talking pretty freely now that I had lifted the curse from myself. In a moment, Ken would do the same, and at least he and I would be okay. It was great to realize I had survived.

"Good thinking," Ken said.

"Thanks."

"You really are a brain."

I tried to answer. But my legs and arms and body and head seemed to have disappeared. I couldn't see or hear or smell or taste. But I could think. That's about all a brain can do. I guess Ken could make me normal again, if he thought of doing it. But, knowing him, that idea will never rise to the surface of his dim little mind.

Thanks a lot, Ken, you idiot. I hope you do something really stupid to yourself.

HIDE

▼

I've got the only brother in the world who's afraid of cows. I know he's just three, and kids that age aren't much more than sticky little bundles of fear, but cows? Give me a break. It wouldn't be so bad, except our house is right next to a dairy farm. There's a fence at the edge of our backyard. We're on one side—me, Mom, Dad, and screaming Barry—and the cows are on the other. The cows are black and white, like the ones you see in the comics sometimes.

It started the day we moved here. Right after we pulled into the driveway, I went to check out the backyard. As usual, Barry stumbled along behind me. As soon as we got around the house, he screamed so loud I almost broke my back spinning toward him. When Barry screams, I usually get blamed, so I'm pretty quick to shut him up. He was pointing at the fence, his mouth wide open, making no sense at all.

"Aaaaaahhhhhh!!!!"

That's pretty much what it sounded like. I figured there was a bee flying around or something. Mom and Dad were out front, so I couldn't ignore the screams. If they found me standing there while Barry was trying to blow his tonsils out of his throat, I'd probably get a lecture.

"What's wrong?" I asked.

He didn't even look at me. He just kept pointing. Finally, he screamed an actual word. "Inside!"

"Sure. Anything you say, little brother." I picked him up. He was so stiff, it was like carrying an armful of baseball bats. I took him in through the back door and put him down on the kitchen floor. "Look, Mom and Dad are stressed out enough with all this moving stuff. Don't give them any trouble, okay?"

"Cows," Barry said. At least he wasn't shouting. It came out as sort of a whimper.

"Yup, cows," I said.

Twin footsteps echoed through the house as the folks crossed the bare floors and marched into the kitchen.

"Is something wrong?" Mom asked. "Did you do something to your brother, Robert?"

"Nah," I said. "Barry got a little spooked by all the new stuff out there, but it's under control."

"Are you sure?" Dad asked.

"Positive."

That satisfied them. They went back to dealing with the boxes that were stacked all over the place. I looked at Barry. He was still a bit red in the face, and sort of slimy around the nose, but it didn't seem like he was going to start screaming again or pass out or anything.

It got worse after that.

Barry wouldn't go near the backyard if there were any cows in sight. This meant he stayed inside or played in the front most of the time. The cows went to a barn to eat, and they wandered around a bunch of pastures, but there were usually at least a few out back.

Whenever Barry caught sight of them, he'd stand glued in place, point straight ahead, and start screaming "Cows!" or shouting "Inside!" Then I'd have to pick him up, carry him into the house, and find some way to distract him until he calmed down.

I was getting pretty sick of the whole routine.

After about a month of that nonsense, I decided it was time for little brother to get cured of his fears.

It was early in the evening. The sun was just dipping down below the horizon. Mom and Dad were at some sort of dinner thing with the local Lions Club or one of those other groups they belong to.

"Let's go out," I said to Barry.

"Cows?" he asked, looking up at me from the floor where he sat surrounded by plastic building blocks. "Cows, Robert?"

"Come on, there's nothing to worry about." I held out my hand. I figured the longer he stayed calm, the closer I could get him to the cows before he started screaming.

Barry took my hand and we walked out the back door. It was growing pretty dark, which was good. If there were cows, he wouldn't spot them right away.

I didn't see any near the yard, but it looked like there were a dozen or so far off by a tree. "Come on," I said, "let's have an adventure."

"Where?"

"You'll see." I lifted Barry over the fence. He clung to my arm, which made it tough for me to step over the top wire. There were these electric things hooked up to shock the animals if they tried to get across. I didn't know how much of a jolt they gave, but I sure didn't want to find out.

We got about halfway to the cluster of cows before Barry caught on.

"Inside!"

"No way, pal," I said, tightening my grip on his hand. "It's time for you to face your fears. Someday, you'll thank me for this."

He dug in. But I was tired of all his tantrums and screaming, so I just dragged him along. It's nice being bigger and stronger. He screamed all the way. I was afraid someone would come running from the farmhouse, but it was far off beyond the pasture. It was pretty much just Barry and me and the cows.

"There's nothing to be scared of," I said, shouting loud enough so maybe he would hear me over his screams. "They're cows—that's all. They don't even eat meat. They're just stupid, smelly cows."

"Inside!" Barry screamed.

We were right in the middle of the group of cows now. In the dark, they looked like big, harmless hunks of beef. Most of them were standing. A couple were sprawled on the ground. I'd had it with the screaming. "Look," I said to Barry. Then I kicked one of the cows. It was like kicking a leather couch. The stupid animal didn't even glance over at me.

"See?" I said. "Nothing to be scared of." I kicked it again.

My plan wasn't working. Barry was so freaked he was making these almost silent screams now. It sounded like when I've pulled the neck of a balloon and let the air squeak out, but it was the squeak that comes at the very end, after most of the pressure is gone. "Face it, kid—we're standing here until you get over this."

That's when I heard it—that ripping sound. But it wasn't a dry rip, like cloth. It was a wet rip.

Barry gasped. Then he got real quiet. He wasn't even trying to scream anymore. That scared me.

I looked to my left as another ripping sound came from the cow next to me. Then there was a wet dripping sound. Then a splashing splat, like five pounds of cottage cheese dropping to the ground.

"Inside," Barry said. He said it quietly. He pointed to the cow.

Something under the cow, something that had dropped from it to the ground, started to stir.

It slithered away from beneath the cow.

The cow fell to its knees, then rolled on its side. It didn't move at all after that.

The thing crawled toward us.

"Inside," Barry said. He turned and pointed to another cow behind us.

Rip.

Then again to the right.

Rip.

That wet sound, dropping from inside the cow, was repeating all around us. I looked at the cow in front of me. In the dim light, I could see the claws and the arm that ripped through from inside. I could see the thing wriggle and crawl out into the world.

They started coming closer.

Barry looked up at me. His eyes seemed calm now. "I told you."

The last of the cows fell. The things from inside moved toward us. They were too wet and shiny to be seen clearly. But they had teeth. Not cow teeth. Not flat teeth for chewing grass, but predator teeth. They didn't move fast, but I wasn't going to wait to see what would happen if they reached us.

As I started to step away, the closest one leaped at me. It hit my stomach, digging claws into my shirt. I slapped at it as I felt a sting in my flesh. My slap was hard enough to knock the thing off.

I turned to run.

I made it to the fence and into our yard before I realized I'd left Barry behind. I stood there, panting, shivering. I started to climb over the fence again, but I couldn't. There was no way I was going back near those things. Whatever my parents might do to me, it couldn't be worse than what those things probably wanted to do. I didn't know what they were, or how Barry could tell they were inside the cows. But I knew I wasn't going back.

I looked down at my shirt. It was ripped, but not too badly. I felt my stomach. There was only a small scratch. I'd been lucky.

Beyond the fence, I saw something moving.

Could it be?

Even in the dark, I knew that walk.

"Barry?" I half whispered it.

He kept walking toward me. He got closer. He reached the fence. I stretched over, grabbed him under the arms, and lifted him. "You okay?" I asked as I set him down on the ground. He seemed fine—no scratches on his skin or tears in his clothing. Maybe he was too small for them to bother with. Suddenly, I realized I might get out of this without any kind of trouble.

Barry looked up and took a step away from me.

"You okay?" I asked again. He wasn't talking, but I guess I could understand him being quiet after the scare he'd had. "You can see those things somehow, can't you? You could tell they were in the cows, right?"

He took another step back.

"Come on, it's over. Let's go."

Barry lifted his arm. He pointed at me. "Inside," he said, pointing his finger straight at my stomach. "Inside Robert." He stared at me for a moment, his eyes filled with a mix of fear and sorrow. Then he turned and ran.

WHERE DOES ALL THIS STUFF COME FROM?

Story ideas come from all over, and they come in many different ways. If I cut myself shaving, I usually bleed a story or two. If someone says something unusual, or does something strange, it can give me a plot. At times, it's something very *ordinary* that can inspire a story. Here's a look at the story behind the stories in this collection.

Fairy in a Jar

Some ideas pop up out of nowhere. This one came to me in the shower. I was struck by the thought of a kid hunting fireflies and catching a fairy. I got dressed and ran to the computer. The whole story poured out in less than an hour. It was the first really good horror story I ever wrote.

The Touch

A friend complained that his daughter lost everything she touched. He suggested I write a story about it. I did, though I don't think the result is what he expected.

At the Wrist

I keep an idea file where I put anything that might make a good story. One entry said: a boy loses his father's hand and it comes back to punish him. It came out wonderfully wacky. This is easily my silliest story.

Crizzles

No idea where it came from. Must have been something I ate.

Light as a Feather, Stiff as a Board

I saw kids playing this game at a picnic. I really wanted something magical to happen. When life doesn't give you what you want, you can write your own ending instead.

The Evil Tree

When I wrote the opening sentence, I had no idea where the story was going. I do that a lot. I end up with tons of unused openings, but I also get lots of stories that way. It's sort of like doodling with words.

Kidzilla

There's a famous short story by Franz Kafka called "Metamorphosis." It's about a man who turns into a disgusting insect. Someone jokingly suggested I should write about a kid who becomes a cockroach. I thought a lizard would be a lot more fun. I started with the opening sentence, and just followed it wherever it wanted to go.

Everyone's a Winner

My daughter and I went wild one day playing skee ball at an amusement park. We ended up winning so many of these little stuffed turtles that we couldn't carry them. They just kept spilling from our clutches. That image was the seed for the story.

A Little Off the Top

The setting and discomfort come straight from childhood memories. I really didn't like going to the barber when I was a kid. My wife cuts my hair now.

The Slide

True story—I was sitting next to a tube slide when a kid came out. He hit the ground—*plock*— and froze for an instant as if he'd just been dropped into the world. Then he looked around and went running off. Some day I guess I'd better confess to the kid's dad that his son inspired such a gruesome story.

Big Kids

This sprang from memories of the fear of Big Kids, combined with a thirst for revenge. Bullies beware—the kid you're messing with today might grow up to be a writer.

Your Worst Nightmare

As a game, my daughter used to try to avoid falling maple leaves. Why avoid them? I wondered. The answer that came to mind was wonderfully shivery.

Phone Ahead

I got the idea for the phone first, then thought up a story about it.

Sand Sharks

I wrote the opening scene with no idea where it would go. But I guess I had sharks on my mind.

On the Road

Memories, again. Those trips sure did seem to stretch out.

The Languages of Beasts

I had the idea for the ending. I like stories that end with a twist, but it's important to plant little hints and clues along the way. Otherwise you end up with a long joke instead of a short story. Luckily, my editor works very hard to keep that from happening.

Class Trip

Another story taken from my idea file. Again, all I really started with was the ending.

Collared

I wish I knew where this one came from. I think it's one of my scariest stories. As far as I remember, I just started writing, making it up as I went along.

The Substitute

Usually, it's the substitute who has a hard time. I thought it might be fun to write about a substitute who isn't quite what he seemed to be. As for Jane, if she's in your class, you might want to think about being a bit nicer to her. You never know . . . .

The Vampire's Rat

I'd been working on a novel about a plague, so I guess I had rats on my mind. At first, I thought this story would be about a disease, but the way it ended up was a lot more shivery.

Slugs

I'd been discussing slugs with a friend (doesn't everyone?), and the story idea just sort of grew from our conversation and a comment she made. I have neat friends.

Snakeland

I've always been fascinated by tourist attractions, especially those small roadside places that are run by one person or a family. They're such a wonderful part of the American highway. I've never been to a place exactly like Snakeland, but I know it's out there waiting for me.

Burger and Fries

This began with an idea of how someone could run a business while cutting down on expenses. Once I had that initial unappetizing concept, the fast-food connection just seemed natural.

Game Over

This might be a case of biting the hand that fed me since I worked for many years as a game designer. But you have to admit, video games have a way of taking over.

Smunkies

A good chunk of my allowance used to go for stuff from mail order catalogs when I was a kid.

The moment I sent in my money, I started watching for the package. You can get some absolutely fabulous junk this way.

Pretty Polly

I know parrots are wonderful creatures. They're colorful, entertaining, and intelligent, but there's something about them that strikes me as a bit sinister.

Join the Party

I suspect most of us have, at some point, looked around and wondered why everything seemed so easy for everyone else. We only know our own fears and weaknesses; We know ourselves from the inside. We see others from the outside. I think most of us are more alike than we realize.

The Billion Legger

In general, I don't mind insects. There's a great spider hanging out in my office right now. I leave it alone. But centipedes make me just a tiny bit uncomfortable. That's a lie—they make me *very* uncomfortable.

The Battle-Ax

There's something frightening and fascinating about old weapons. They almost seem to have a power of their own.

In the Land of the Lawn Weenies

I like to go for a walk every day. It's a good way to get ideas. One afternoon, as I strolled through the neighborhood, I noticed a lot of people out mowing their lawns. It almost made me feel I was living in a hive, where all the workers were functioning by instinct.

Sunburn

I'd started out wanting to write something about a couple of kids who go overboard trying to get a tan. The story took a twist I didn't expect, but I like the way it turned out.

Thin Silk

One evening, I walked into a whole bunch of thin strands of spider web. They seemed to be everywhere that night. I brushed them away, but the idea stuck.

The Witch's Monkey

My daughter loves cats. She has cat shirts, cat jewelry (especially earrings), cat sheets, cat books, cat posters, and tons of other feline things. I took this passion, transferred it to a more unusual animal, and let the story grow from there.

As You Say

This started out with the idea for the curse. I didn't know when I began that it would take off in such a wacky direction, but that's part of the fun. One of the joys of writing is that there are no limits.

Hide

My daughter's friend Amanda lives in a house with a lovely view. Her backyard borders a farm. It's hard to stand there and enjoy that peaceful scene without getting an idea or two.

Well, that's it for this collection. I'd like to stick around, but I've been thinking about these piles of leaves I saw on my last walk. There's a story in them. It's sort of a wild idea, but I think I can turn it into a good tale. Guess I'd better get back to work.

ABOUT THE AUTHOR

David Lubar grew up in Morristown, New Jersey, spent a few years in Northern California, and ended up, much to his delight, in Eastern Pennsylvania. He likes writing short stories and hates mowing his lawn. Though he's never owned a monkey, a smunkie, a rat, or a parrot, he does live near an awful lot of cows. His first novel, *Hidden Talents,* is an American Library Association "Best Books for Young Adults" selection. He lives in Pennsylvania with his wife and daughter.